FIRST COME, FIRST KILL

When a mysterious woman visited Gregory Payne, warning him of danger, he dismissed her. Shortly afterwards, he was dead . . . His grieving daughter Linda arrives home with her new husband Walter Gordon, to be greeted by private detective John Storm, who believes Gregory to have been murdered. The dead man left money to various beneficiaries besides Linda — a faithful servant, an old friend, a dissolute cousin, and a steadfast godfather. Could one of them have been moved to strike him down?

SPECIAL MESSAGE TO READERS

THE ULVERSCROFT FOUNDATION
(registered UK charity number 264873)

was established in 1972 to provide funds for research, diagnosis and treatment of eye diseases. Examples of major projects funded by the Ulverscroft Foundation are:-

- The Children's Eye Unit at Moorfields Eye Hospital, London
- The Ulverscroft Children's Eye Unit at Great Ormond Street Hospital for Sick Children
- Funding research into eye diseases and treatment at the Department of Ophthalmology, University of Leicester
- The Ulverscroft Vision Research Group, Institute of Child Health
- Twin operating theatres at the Western Ophthalmic Hospital, London
- The Chair of Ophthalmology at the Royal Australian College of Ophthalmologists

You can help further the work of the Foundation by making a donation or leaving a legacy. Every contribution is gratefully received. If you would like to help support the Foundation or require further information, please contact:

**THE ULVERSCROFT FOUNDATION
The Green, Bradgate Road, Anstey
Leicester LE7 7FU, England
Tel: (0116) 236 4325
website: www.foundation.ulverscroft.com**

FRANCIS K. ALLAN

$\blacklozenge$

FIRST COME, FIRST KILL

Complete and Unabridged

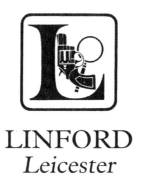

LINFORD
Leicester

First published in Great Britain

First Linford Edition
published 2019

A catalogue record for this book is available
from the British Library.

ISBN 978–1–4448–4169–5

Published by
F. A. Thorpe (Publishing)
Anstey, Leicestershire

Set by Words & Graphics Ltd.
Anstey, Leicestershire
Printed and bound in Great Britain by
T. J. International Ltd., Padstow, Cornwall

This book is printed on acid-free paper

1

'There, Walt! There's a parking place,' the girl said as the car turned into Lower Broadway in Manhattan. 'I'll only be a few minutes. If I don't go up and see him, he'll have a tantrum.' She opened the door of the coupé.

'Wait,' the man said. He turned the key and got out beside her. 'You don't mind if I come along?'

A faintly puzzled frown crossed the girl's forehead. She shook her head and smiled. 'How long will it last?'

'Will what last?' He looked at her curiously.

'Your constant devotion, darling.' She laughed. 'We've been married four days, and I don't think I've been out of your sight four minutes the whole time.'

'Oh. That.' That was all he said, yet his voice held a vague suspension, an unfinished quality. The girl stopped and looked at him. It had been there again, she realized: a metallic gleam in his dark eyes, a hardening line down his jaw.

They entered an elevator and left it at the tenth floor. The girl moved with a rhythmic swinging stride, even and free. Her head was bare and the waves of her golden-brown hair swayed to her movements. She wore a wrinkled woolen skirt, a tan sweater, and a short-sleeved leather jacket. Her brown eyes were tinted with the gold of her hair. A pair of sunglasses swung lazily in her fingers. The tall man's hair was short-cropped and black, crisply waving. His eyes were black and arresting, with a faintest hint of irony in them when he smiled. Now they were alert and intense as he watched the girl, the doors, the corridor along which they moved.

She paused and opened a door which bore the title:

Gabriel, Mintz and McCormack:
Attorneys-at-Law

'Hello,' she said. An elderly, gaunt-figured woman looked up from the reception desk. 'Do we wait or go in?'

'Oh, good afternoon, Miss Payne! But it's Mrs. Gordon, isn't it?' She laughed thinly. 'You may go in, Mr. Gabriel is in his office.'

'Thank you.' The girl turned toward the inner corridor. The man followed.

They entered a large room of dark pine ceiling and massive leather furnishings. Row on row of thick books filled the wall-cases, and the gray haze of cigar smoke sifted slowly through the air.

'Hello, Uncle Gabe!' the girl said cheerfully.

'Uh?' At the wide desk across the room, a thick-shouldered and florid-faced man raised his mane of gray hair. He tugged his half-moon glasses down from his forehead. 'Who is . . . ? Well!'

Gabriel heaved himself from the chair and yanked down his vest as he rounded the desk with an elephantine swagger. He gathered in the girl's hand and kissed it resoundingly.

'When did you get back, Linda?' he demanded.

'This very minute. We picked up the car where I'd left it in Newark. We're on the way to the house now.'

'We?' Gabriel backed off and lowered his briar-like brows to peer at the man for the first time.

'Why, Uncle Gabe! You remember Walter Gordon? And I wrote you that — you haven't even read my letter!'

'Letter?' He plunged his hands into his pockets. 'Well . . . Gordon, you say?' He turned toward the tall young man. 'Seems I remember you now. Play a fiddle, don't you?'

'The piano.' A dry smile crossed Gordon's lips. 'It probably makes little difference.'

'If you'd read my letter,' Linda said, 'you'd have known that we were married four days ago in New Mexico.'

'Married, you say?' Gabriel revolved violently to face her. He blinked and his sharp bushy glance darted back to Walt. 'Well, I must say!'

'Don't you approve?' Linda asked edgily.

'Approve?' He snorted. 'My dear child, I'm too old to give a damn!'

'Perhaps,' Gordon said, 'a good lawyer

would advise his client against marrying a musician?'

A wide smile unraveled itself across the lawyer's mouth. 'Young man, a lawyer as old as I am will advise against anything. Including,' he said, reaching forward to tap Walter's chest with a fat finger, 'listening to an old man talk.' He smiled, and faced Linda again. 'What are you going to do now?'

'We're going up to the house. I came by to say hello and to see if you'd contacted Goode. When I wrote you, I asked you to call him.'

'Goode . . . ? Oh, your father's man. Seems I heard Miss Tate saying something about it yesterday. You ask her.' He frowned. 'Going back up there . . . ?'

'Is there any reason why we shouldn't?' Charles Gabriel had always had a talent for making Linda impatient; today he seemed more adept that usual.

'Oh, no! None at all. No sane reason for allowing the past to shadow the present, as I say.' He moved back toward his desk to get his frayed cigar. 'I want to have a talk with you,' he said vaguely. He

5

chewed the cigar as he surveyed his littered desk. 'Been a few things I don't like,' he muttered. 'Can't put my finger where, exactly. I . . . Ever heard of a man named John Storm?' he asked abruptly.

'John Storm?' Linda shook her head.

'I don't like him,' Gabriel snapped, frowning. 'Can't make out what he's up to, prowling around, asking questions, waving a check he says your father gave him. I don't like . . . Well, we'll settle all that later.' He smiled. 'Tell you what: I'll try to get out and see you tomorrow. Tomorrow's Sunday.'

'Fine.' Linda gave him a smile. 'We've got to be going now. I'll speak to Miss Tate.' She opened the door. Just as she turned, she saw Walter's eyes. They were glowing with a half-amused dry mockery as they studied Gabriel. The expression vanished as he turned to follow her a moment later.

At the reception desk, Linda said: 'Miss Tate, I wonder if — '

The gaunt, elderly woman was already nodding assent. 'I knew Mr. Gabriel would let it slip his mind. I called Goode yesterday. He said everything would be ready.'

'Thank you!'

'I just have to say something,' Miss Tate broke out as Linda reached for the door. 'You just can't imagine how I felt, what it really meant to all of us. Your father was just such a gentleman! An old-school gentleman, Mrs. Gordon.'

'Thank you so much, Miss Tate. I know he would — '

'I wanted so much to do something really nice, but you feel so helpless, don't you? I did send flowers, but it all just seemed so . . . Oh, just so tragic, if you understand! Mr. Payne, of all people! And — '

'Yes, of course,' Linda breathed tensely. She wrenched open the door and stumbled into the outer hall. A moment later Walter joined her. Her fingers clenched.

'I guess people as a whole aren't very sensitive, darling,' he said quietly. 'You can't let it get to you. There'll be more like her.'

They entered the elevator. Linda

watched the floors slide past. Automatically she stepped out and followed Walter across the lobby and back to the car. The motor started and he turned into the stream of traffic moving up Broadway.

'I suppose the reason it hurts is because I can't understand, Walt,' Linda said at last. 'Why did he do it? Why?' she echoed blankly. 'There wasn't one single reason!'

Her husband reached over to clasp her tense fingers. 'Whatever his reasons were, you'll know when the time comes.'

She turned to look at him. 'Something in the way you said that,' she began strangely, 'it was almost as if you knew something — '

'You're letting your nerves get away from you, Linda,' he said quietly.

She sighed and leaned back. 'I know,' she agreed finally. 'I try to forget. I tell myself he did have a good reason. I tell myself he never believed in worrying; he wouldn't want me to act this way. I tell myself a hundred things, and yet . . . '

She took a deep breath and made her tense fingers relax. She made herself see Broadway and the crowds weaving on the walks. She felt the warmth of sunlight on her arm. 'It'll be pretty. It's always pretty in summer,' she said quietly.

Forty minutes later and some twenty miles above New York City, Walt turned the coupé off the highway that trailed the Hudson River. A gravel driveway led through a high, unkempt hedge. With the first sharp curve within the wall of hedge, the world of smooth concrete, cars, and the Hudson River vanished entirely.

The driveway, really a trail, roamed its way through a weeded and wooded field, gradually approaching a house whose high white columns shone in the afternoon sunlight. From the field, birds rose in frantic flight. She saw the hothouse, her father's tulips.

Linda breathed deeply. She knew the scent — the scent of grass, of dust and weeds in warm sunlight. Eagerly, her eyes took in the scene about her. She felt, in strange detachment, that she was returning here after an immeasurable interlude. Time, in this last week, had lost its shape and balance in her mind. Yet now, as the car moved slowly closer to the house, a pattern seemed to form out of nowhere, to settle gently and comfortably about her.

This was home, the place where she was born, the place where her mother had died — so long ago that Linda could hardly remember. This was the world where she and her father had lived. This *was* her father, in breath and spirit.

He was in the silence, in the remote withdrawal from the world beyond the hedge-wall. A tree with two rotting strands of rope dangling from a limb swept her back to the day her father had climbed that tree and made a swing. That was but one thing. In the house, each room was the same — full with signs pointing back into memory.

And now, though she knew he was gone, she felt the spirit of him drawing warm and close about her, blending from the scent of his fields and waiting within the walls of his house. For Linda, time had ceased to be. The present was gone. She was back somewhere in a magic day of the past, and nothing at all was changed.

The car stopped. Abruptly, Linda

awoke to reality and glanced at Walt.

'I was just thinking — ' she began apologetically.

'I know what you were thinking.' He leaned over and kissed her.

'Welcome, Miss Linda,' a thin voice said. She turned. In the doorway, a rigid smile on his grayish lips, stood the ancient figure of Goode, Linda's father's man-of-all-work. 'And you, sir,' he added to Walt.

'Hello, Goode.' Linda got out and extended her hand. The old man achieved a moment of warmth as he touched her fingers.

'I rather hoped you'd come back, Miss,' he said. He straightened. 'I've prepared the middle north room. I'll have the bags up at once.'

Linda nodded. Walt followed her into the cool, shadowy hall that extended down the center of the house to the wide, curving stairway. Her eyes hurried over the light plaster walls, to the high ceilings with their dark-bladed, old-fashioned fans. The scent of the house was the same — the scent of coolness and space and quiet.

Suddenly Linda wanted to be everywhere, in every room, touching and seeing everything, reassuring herself that this, at least, remained unchanged. Then her eyes moved slowly toward the curving stairway. She felt her feet move. It was as though some invisible cord were drawing her slowly yet relentlessly forward and up.

Her fingers slipped along the banister rail. She climbed. She turned at the landing and the wide hall of the second floor stretched out before her toward the front of the house. Her feet carried her on, on to a door that was closed. She touched the knob and felt the latch yield.

Walt was beside her, his hand touching her arm.

'Don't you think — ' he began.

She shook her head. 'I want to see it now, just as it was.'

The door swung slowly inward, opening up before her the room that had been her father's. She stood there looking, unmoving.

Across the expanse of blue rug the sun was stretching. In the corner across the room was her father's writing desk. In its place with its back toward her was the rigid chair that matched the dark wood of the desk. The drawers of the desk were toward her, all neatly closed now. Upon the desk was his pen-set, a leather-bound blotter, a small photograph of herself, an empty vase of bronze.

Silently she entered the room. Opposite the desk was the closet. The door was ajar, and Linda saw his suits hanging there; a gray suit, a blue suit — she remembered them all. In another corner was his bed, spread with a yellow cover. In the center of the room was a sagging rocker with an ashtray built into the arm. A low bookcase ran beneath the triple windows that looked toward the north.

Slowly she moved to the bed. She touched the yellow cover, strangely immaculate and smooth.

'There . . . Right there,' she whispered. 'One week ago today, there . . . my father killed himself . . . '

'No more, Linda,' Walt urged. 'We can come back.' He tried to turn her toward the door. She did not move. Her eyes moved on about the room. They halted on the bookcase.

'One of his books is gone!' she said. 'One of the Encyclopedia volumes.'

'We'll find it. Perhaps it's downstairs. We — '

'The desk!' she whispered. 'Look! That wasn't there before.' She touched a deep, thin scar in the dark polished wood. 'It looks almost like . . . like a knife had — '

'Linda. Come on. You can see this room later.' Walt's words were blunt to the point of impatience.

She glanced at him in surprise. He gestured abruptly toward the hall. 'Come on.'

'But, Walt, I just want to see — ' She stared at him, feeling the breath drain from her throat. 'You . . . What is it? There's something — '

'We're hungry. We're both tired. Let's eat. We can come back here then.' He took her hand firmly and drew her from the room, closing the door behind them.

At that moment Goode came out of the adjoining room toward the front of the house.

'It's all ready, Miss. I'll have something

14

prepared when you come down.'

Walt waited until the man had vanished down the stairs, then he and Linda entered the bedroom. He stood in the center of the room, his hands in his pockets, a half-smile playing at the corners of his mouth.

'Darling, this is almost indecent,' he said lightly. 'We're spending a honeymoon in a room that's practically a nursery. Those things on the wallpaper are bunnies, so help me.'

'Oh.' Linda colored, then she laughed. 'Goode wasn't thinking.'

'That was nice of Goode.' Walt pulled off his coat. 'Do me a favor and start a shower,' he said suddenly. 'I want to make a call.' He left the room and closed the door, but the latch did not catch and it swung ajar.

Linda heard his steps halt at the telephone table near the head of the stairs. She went into the bathroom. Just as she began turning the knobs of the shower, she heard his muted voice:

' . . . want to speak to John Storm at Carlisle 4-4359 in New York City, please.'

The first drops of water were splashing from the shower. Abruptly Linda remembered: John Storm, that was the name Gabriel had mentioned. A man snooping around, asking questions . . .

Slowly she turned the knobs off. The water ceased splashing. She stood still.

'Storm . . . ?' Walt's soft words reached her ears. 'This is Gordon . . . Yes, we're out here now . . . No, everything's perfectly all right. Nothing happened the entire time. I was with her all the time . . . Yes, but . . . No, Storm. You better come out tonight . . . Tonight. I can't deceive her much longer . . . Well, not exactly, but she saw the desk. She knows a book is missing. She has a suspicion, perhaps . . . Yes, tonight. Early . . . Goodbye, Storm.'

Linda heard the receiver set down in its cradle. She heard Walt's footsteps returning along the hall. Quickly she turned the knobs, and the water poured noisily from the shower. A moment later Walt was in the bedroom.

'That's going to feel good after that train,' he announced cheerfully. He whistled as he pulled off his shirt. He took off his shoes and wandered into the bathroom. 'Love me?' He leaned over and kissed her throat.

Slowly he straightened. 'Something got your tongue, darling?'

'Tongue?' she said absently. 'Oh, nothing.' She pulled her eyes from his probing gaze. Her fingers slipped along her sun-tanned throat. 'I think I'll change clothes.' She turned from the bathroom. Walt closed the door halfway, and she heard the rings of the shower-curtain slide along the rod.

She stood quite still in the center of the room, her eyes speculatively on the half-open door. She felt the slow throb of the pulse in her throat, felt her breasts rise and fall to her slow deep breathing. And in her mind she heard again the words:

'I can't deceive her much longer . . . she saw the desk . . . She has a suspicion, perhaps . . . '

And as she stood there, she felt it again — an indefinable sensation, an intangible uncertainty. It had come and come again, always fleeting, in this last week. And it left her with a breath of anxiety stirring in her throat. Something was wrong, she knew. It was focused in Walt — in his words, his eyes. In the way —

Suddenly she shook her head and closed her eyes.

'Stop it! Stop it!' she whispered harshly to herself. 'That's my husband! I love him. I've got to stop thinking until . . . '

2

They ate dinner on the glass-enclosed sunporch at the back of the house. From the windows could be seen the garage, with Goode's quarters above. From the sunporch, a gravel path led off across the back lawn, then vanished into a sharp ravine that broke down to a narrow, winding stream. The path reappeared as it climbed the opposite side of the ravine and twisted its way into a wooded field toward the east. From the south windows of the porch, a dark fragment of the Hudson River was visible as it flowed down to the Atlantic.

They ate quietly. From time to time, Linda started conversation. Walt answered absently. His dark eyes were thoughtful and remote. A dozen times she found him gazing into space, his body utterly still and the food before him forgotten.

From the front hall came the ringing of the telephone. Linda heard Goode's steps leave the kitchen. Presently he returned.

'Was that anyone for us?'

The man appeared. 'It was rather odd, Miss. Some gentleman wished to know if you were home. When I replied, he hung up. He left no name or message.'

Walt looked up quickly. 'You said we were here?'

'Yes, sir. That is, I said that Miss Linda was. I had no time to explain further.' He hesitated a moment. 'I mentioned it as odd because the same thing happened last evening, Miss.'

'Someone called yesterday?' Walt's question was sharp, abrupt.

Goode blinked anxiously as he nodded. 'You see, I arrived here about four yesterday afternoon to prepare for Miss Linda and you. And about seven o'clock a gentleman's voice called to inquire if Miss Linda were in. Just as tonight, he hung up immediately when I replied.' Goode looked uneasily at Walt. 'I hope there was nothing wrong in what I — '

'Oh, no. Of course not,' Walt interrupted. 'Nothing at all.'

'Linda! Damn you, darling!' a rich

baritone voice shouted.

She turned, startled. Out of the ravine and past the hothouse moved a mass of colors. It leaped up the steps and swept across the sunporch. It resolved itself into a large blond man. His arms closed about her and his lips came down on hers. 'Damn, it's good to see you, darling!'

'I'm glad to see you, Glenn,' Linda returned breathlessly. Her eyes swept over his checkered polo coat, his stained yellow corduroy slacks, and sweatshirt of faded crimson. His hair was thick and blond and curly. A trim, pale mustache traced his upper lip, and his sunken blue eyes danced brightly.

'I suppose you've been back for days,' he accused poutingly.

'Just today. We . . . Oh, you know Walt, don't you? Glenn Darby, my cousin, Walt.'

'Walt? Oh hell, yes!' Glenn agreed heartily, turning toward Walt for the first time. 'Glad to see you. Musician, aren't you?'

Walt smiled slightly as he nodded. 'Dramatist, aren't you?'

'Ah, scorn enters your voice. I forgive you immediately. And I anticipate your next question: No, I have neither written nor produced anything of late, thank God. I . . . Ah, Goode! Glad to see you,' he said as the man came out of the kitchen. 'Do you suppose there'd be just the least bit of scotch and water around?'

'You've eaten?' Linda asked quickly.

'Horribly. Just the scotch and water, darling.' He sat down and lit a cigarette. 'Just luck that I took a walk and saw the light in the kitchen here, and like the bad moth I come to the flame. Ah, splendid, Goode!' Glenn leaned forward to mix a drink. 'By the way, how long will you be here, Linda?' he asked.

'How long? Why, I'm going to stay. It's home.'

'Oh.' Glenn hesitated a moment to glance at her across the rim of the glass. With one swift motion he drained the drink and returned the glass to the table. 'I don't . . . didn't know,' he said.

A silence filled the sunporch as Glenn filled his glass again.

'You're still living at the summerhouse?'

Linda asked to make conversation.

'The summerhouse?' He looked at her and smiled wryly. 'You were always the epitome of tact. Yes, I am still living in the remodeled servants' quarters, my dear.'

Again the silence. Glenn drained his glass. 'Oh, come! When did the myth of my finances cause such a pall? You used to joke about it. You're changing and I don't like it!' He laughed but the sound was hollow. His lips straightened into a tired line as he filled the glass a third time. 'Well, up and over . . . This is to my fun and yours, and for God's sake laugh!'

He emptied the glass. No one laughed. Linda glanced mutely at Walt.

'I wish you wouldn't, darling,' Glenn said suddenly, very softly.

'You wish I wouldn't what?' Linda asked.

'Stay here. I'm afraid. You can't understand that,' he said slowly. And now his voice had lost its hearty bravado and banter.

Linda's brows arched. 'What do you mean, Glenn?'

'Mean?' His fixed gaze moved to her

eyes. And Linda found his eyes suddenly haggard, fevered. 'I don't know,' he said vacantly. He poured another drink and swallowed it jerkily.

'What the devil are you talking about?' Walt demanded.

Darby looked at him and shook his head. 'You wouldn't understand. You have to . . . to be so afraid that you are paralyzed. You can only sit and wait. You have to be so afraid that the fear is a poison in you, eating all the time — like a sore on the edge of your heart and your brain — making you into nothing! You can't fight! You — '

'Glenn!' Linda cried. 'Don't talk that way! I — '

'I beg pardon, Miss,' Goode spoke quietly. 'A gentleman is waiting in the study. A Mr. John Storm.'

'Oh.' Linda straightened suddenly. Walt rose.

'You've got to excuse us, Darby,' he said curtly.

'Please come back some other time,' Linda said.

Glenn Darby did not speak. His lips

24

were parted. His eyes were wide. His body was as tense as steel, and a pulse hammered in his temple. He was facing the doorway where Goode had stood. He did not move or speak as they left him.

'I don't like your cousin, darling,' Walt whispered as they moved along the hall to the front of the house. 'He's a fool.'

'I know. But a pathetic fool. I'm very sorry for him.'

They paused at the closed door of the study. There, Walt touched her hand. 'Just a moment,' he said quietly. He was frowning and his dark eyes were troubled. 'This is going to be hard,' he said gently. 'Maybe I should have done part of it, but . . . I couldn't,' he said emptily. 'Just take it as easily as you can. Listen to what Storm says. You can believe and trust him.'

Before Linda could speak, Walt opened the door. They entered the long dark-paneled room. From a window, a man turned to face them. He smiled and came forward.

He was slender. He moved quietly. His hair was brown and his clothes were undistinctive. Then he came into the brighter range of the lamplight, and his face was clearly revealed. Linda looked at him intently.

In the first moment, his face seemed utterly plain. Then it seemed to develop, though not a muscle moved. In the brown eyes there was keen intensity. Flecks of gray showed in the brown hair. A fragile vibrance seemed to radiate, to stir restlessly beneath the calm surface of his features. Instinctively and at once, Linda knew that this person was a stranger in her know-ledge of men, and she could not draw her eyes from the flexible mask of his calm face.

'Good evening, Mr. Gordon,' he said. 'And Mrs. Gordon. I've never had the pleasure before. I am John Storm.'

'Good evening,' Linda said. They shook hands.

'I hope you enjoyed your vacation — what there was of it.'

'I did. Naturally it was much shorter than . . . '

'Much shorter than we had hoped,' Storm supplied quietly as Linda hesitated.

'Won't you sit down, please?'

Walt moved another chair closer to the lamp. Linda sat down beside him, both of them facing Storm. He too sat down, and laid his cigarettes and matches on the tray beside the chair. A few silent moments passed as he lit a cigarette, then he looked from Linda to Walt.

'You are wondering why I'm here,' he began. 'I'll begin by saying that I am a member of that strange breed known as private detectives. Usually people know little about us until they have to learn under unfortunate circumstances. I'm sorry you're not an exception.' He paused. 'I'll try to tell this as simply as I can, Mrs. Gordon. What I have to say concerns work I began at the instance of your father. Now, and more importantly, it concerns you.

'Sixteen days ago, on the Thursday evening of May fourth, a woman came to this house. Goode, as usual, was away; you were in Warburn at the movies with Mr. Gordon. Your father was alone. This woman arrived without introduction, completely unknown to your father. She

27

refused to identify herself. She asked him to pay her five thousand dollars. In return she promised to reveal certain facts, the nature of which she would not disclose then. However, she said that this information would probably save your life, Mrs. Gordon. And without it, she stated, you would almost surely die very soon.'

'You . . . You mean — ' Linda gasped. Walt touched her arm.

'Let me finish before we consider any questions,' Storm suggested quietly. 'Your father was furious, outraged at the idea of blackmail. He ordered the woman from the house immediately. She obeyed promptly. But, as she left, she warned him that he too might be in danger. She said she would contact him again. And then she made a curious request. She begged him to keep her visit a secret from any of his friends, even though he decided to notify the police of her call. No friend of his was to know.' Storm paused.

'When the woman had gone, your father's anger passed. As he reflected, it seemed to him that there had been a sincerity in the woman's voice. And it seemed that she had been nervous and apprehensive, though not toward your father — toward something else, some other, outside source. The more your father thought, the more concerned and curious he became. And he was a cautious man. He regretted his anger. He decided that he would see the woman if she called again.

'She telephoned him from New York the next morning. Your father told her to return. She agreed, with certain precautions. She instructed him to be alone between the hours of eight and ten each evening for the next four nights; on one of those nights she would visit him. And once again she carefully warned him to tell none of his friends of her, even though he had called the police. She asked if he had spoken of her; your father said he hadn't. That was Friday.' Storm paused to put out his cigarette. Linda forced herself to breathe deeply, to relax. Walt stirred slightly.

'The woman never appeared,' Storm continued. 'On the following Sunday morning, the seventh, Goode discovered a piece of jewelry — a shoulder ornament — in the driveway. He took it to your father. Mr. Payne recognized it as an ornament that the woman had been wearing when she first came here. He accompanied Goode to the driveway. There in the soft earth at the edge of the drive were the prints of a woman's shoes. They led from the highway, along the edge of the drive, to the place where Goode had found the pin, the ornament. After that there were no more. But on the pebbles of the drive, near the last shoe-prints, your father found stains of blood.' Storm was silent for a moment.

'There were no other footprints?' Walt asked suddenly.

'None in the field or on the edge of the drive. If there were any on the driveway, the loose gravel concealed them. Mr. Payne felt sure that the woman had tried to reach him, probably the evening before. Someone, something, he assumed, had stopped her at that place where her footprints ended and the ornament was found. Something had stopped and injured her,' Storm emphasized, 'for the blood was relatively fresh. And so, at noon that day, he called me. I arrived that afternoon. You, Mrs. Gordon, were in New York at Carnegie Hall. I took your father's description of the woman. I searched this house, the grounds, and probed the creek. I found no trace of the woman. I returned to New York, since it was from New York that she had telephoned your father, from a public station. I attempted to associate her with various missing-persons reports.'

'What was she like?' Linda asked slowly.

'She was a plain woman, without unusual characteristics. She was about forty, brown hair and eyes, rather thin and rigid in posture. There were two things your father remembered most clearly about her. The first was her almost flawless diction, as contrasted with her otherwise ordinary manner and appear-ance. The second was the strong perfume she'd worn that first day she had come here. Lilac-scented, your father said, and used to excess.' Storm lit another cigarette and continued:

'Naturally, such a description was hardly enough. Then I remembered the shoulder ornament. Your father got it for me. It was rather large, shaped to resemble the outspread wings of a butterfly. But the curious thing about the ornament was this: though it was of heavy copper, beautifully hand wrought, and obviously expensive, the settings, about two dozen in number, now held only imitation jade of the cheapest sort. But tiny scars on the settings were discernible, indicating that other stones had been removed and the imitations substituted. Lastly, on the back of the copper mounting, was a single engraved letter — S.

'Well, I took the pin with me into New York. I went to Cartasiere's on Fifth Avenue and had them examine the pin. They told me immediately that it was the work of a famous craftsman named Soresco, formerly of Paris but of New York for the past ten years or so. Whereupon I visited Mr. Soresco in his shop on Lexington Avenue. He does all of his own work, producing quality and not quantity. Furthermore, he possesses a keen memory. As soon as I showed him the ornament, he was able to give me its history. I might add that he was infuriated with the stripping of the original stones. Soresco explained that he had made the pin to order for a Mr. Phillip LeSalle, a wealthy bachelor, seven years ago. The pin was created to be a present for someone; the original stones had been rubies; Mr. LeSalle had designed the butterfly shape himself. So I visited Mr. LeSalle at his Park Avenue apartment.' Storm gestured and leaned slightly forward.

'LeSalle told me the rest of the story. Seven years ago he fancied himself in love with Madame Sio Bido, a half-Japanese prima donna who was then touring this country. *Madame Butterfly* was a part of her repertoire. LeSalle had the pin made for her, gave it to her, but soon drifted on to someone else. He had no idea what had become of Madame Bido or the pin. So, from LeSalle's, I went to government authorities, hoping they might possibly have some record of Madame Bido as an alien. Fortunately they did. She is living in a small hotel on Broadway; she reports regularly to authorities. I visited her. I found her in financial difficulty; the war has destroyed her popularity here. She explained that she had been forced to sell the jewels from the pin. At last, three months ago, she sold the empty mounting for less than two dollars. She remembered the purchaser — a Mr. Verdi Allegretto in Greenwich Village. And so I went to Allegretto's,' Storm said with a weary smile.

'Allegretto recognized the pin. He had set in the imitation jade stones and put the pin in the window of his antique shop. He remembered selling it. A week before, he said, a woman had entered the shop — a brown-haired, brown-eyed woman whose perfume had been strong with the scent of lilac. She had had a cold; your father, too, had spoken of that — '

'The same woman!' Linda exclaimed swiftly.

'The same. She had asked to see the pin. As she inspected it, she murmured something about *Madame Butterfly*.

When Allegretto told her from whom he had purchased the mounting, the woman seemed delighted. Once, she had seen Madame Bido on the street; had recognized her, she said. Madame Bido had been wearing this same pin. The woman wanted it. Allegretto recalled that she had had hardly enough money to buy the pin. But that was the story of the — '

He stopped as the match-flame winked out before he could light another cigarette. He started to strike another match. His movement stilled. Linda saw an expression of almost electric concentration flash across his face. His entire body seemed to freeze. His lips scarcely moved. His words began as a whisper. All of it took hardly a moment.

'Mrs. Gordon, I want you to . . . FALL TO THE FLOOR FAST!' The last words thundered into her face. In the same instant Storm leaped forward. The lamp tilted and crashed to the floor, plunging the room into darkness. Linda obeyed the thunderous command without a moment of thought. Face-forward, she sprawled on the rug.

Then came an angry smashing roar from the darkness across the room. There was a smacking smash against some wall. The roar echoed, shaking the room.

'Down! Stay down, Linda!' Walt shouted in the darkness. She heard his chair crash over.

3

The hall door slammed. Footsteps raced toward the front door. That too slammed wildly. The footsteps pounded on the gravel walk outside. Their furious rhythm faded in the distance and a tense, strained silence filled the darkness of the study.

'Linda? You're not hurt?' Walt whispered breathlessly.

'I'm all right,' she assured him shakily. In the darkness his fingers found hers and tightened. A door closed at the rear of the house and swift steps came padding up the hall.

'Miss Linda?' Goode's high cracking voice called anxiously. 'Where are — '

'In here, Goode,' Walt called softly. 'Stand still. Leave the lights off.' There was a faint gasp, then silence in the hall.

All of it could have taken no more than five minutes, then in the distance, toward the highway, Linda heard a car-motor roaring. She heard tires scream and whine. Slowly the roaring faded in the distance.

'Somebody getting away in a car,' Walt said tensely.

Linda felt him rise in the dark. She got up slowly. Her knees trembled. Gravel crunched on the driveway as footsteps came near. The front door closed solidly.

'Are you all right?' Storm asked sharply. The hall light flashed on, and he appeared in the study doorway. In his hand was a gun.

'Yes, I'm all right. Surprised is all,' Linda said uneasily.

'I heard an explosion, sir,' Goode began nervously.

'Never mind now. You can go,' the detective said. He turned on the overhead light in the study. Goode looked anxiously at Linda. She nodded. The man mopped his gray, lined face as he left.

Storm strode across the study to the long French doors that opened upon the dark terrace. He opened and stepped through one, and knelt down. He straightened and faced into the room, raising his gun and pointing it at an angle.

'Look in that wall, Gordon,' he ordered. Walt followed the line of his arm to the inner wall.

'A hole! Here it is! And the slug's down there!'

'Sit in that same chair, Mrs. Gordon. Just as you were.'

Linda obeyed mutely. Storm sighted down his gun. His lips twitched slightly. Slowly he returned the gun to inside his coat.

'Technically,' he said with a wry smile, 'you can consider yourself dead. Technically, though, a draft from the opened door wasn't supposed to blow out my match.'

He stepped inside the study, slammed and locked the door, and drew all the drapes shut.

'But why did anyone — ?' Linda began breathlessly, her mind finding words again. Storm paid no attention. He was striding back across the study toward the hall.

'Ten o'clock,' he muttered as he glanced at his watch. He disappeared into the hall, and Linda heard Storm give a

New York telephone number to the Warburn operator. She turned toward Walt.

'What does it all mean? Why did — ?'

'I don't know. I'm damned if I know,' he said blankly. He was frowning at the bullet hole. His angry puzzled eyes moved on to the French doors. He shook his head. 'I'm damned if I do.'

'Hello?' Storm's voice sounded in the hall. 'Is Charles Gabriel in?' There was a pause. 'Come here, Mrs. Gordon,' he called. She hurried into the hall. The detective muffled the telephone. 'This is going to be Charles Gabriel. Invite him to midday dinner here tomorrow. It'll be Sunday. He can make it. Be insistent.' He handed her the telephone. Presently the booming voice came through the wire:

'Yes? Gabriel speaking.'

'Uncle Gabe, this is Linda.' She tried to sound calm. 'We wondered if you could come out tomorrow in time for dinner?'

'Dinner? Let me see . . . '

'Ask him,' Storm whispered, 'to bring your father's will.'

'I believe I can make it, my dear,'

Gabriel said. 'Glad to come.'

'Fine. About one o'clock. And, Uncle Gabe, could you bring Father's will with you? I'd like to look it over.'

'Absolutely! Good time to go over the whole arrangement,' he agreed heartily. 'Tell you what: I'll drive out early — say, in the middle of the morning. That'll give us time.'

'Fine. We'll be waiting.' She replaced the receiver and turned to Storm. 'Why did — '

He shook his head, called another number, and handed the receiver back to her. 'This will be Glenn Darby. Ask him to come over late tomorrow afternoon.'

Linda listened to the intermittent ringing. After a full minute Storm broke the connection. His eyes were speculative as he signaled the operator again.

'Argoyle 6-4435,' he said. He handed the telephone back to Linda. 'As the old family doctor, he shouldn't be ignored. Ask him to dinner tomorrow, too,' he suggested wryly.

Presently a woman's voice answered: 'Hello?'

41

'May I speak to Dr. Clifton Shore, please?' Linda asked.

'I'm sorry, but the doctor isn't here. This is Mrs. Shore. Can I take a message?'

'Find out how long he's been gone,' Storm whispered.

'Can you tell me when he left?' Linda asked.

'I believe it was just after nine. He received a telephone call.'

Linda glanced inquiringly at Storm. *Dinner*, his lips said silently. She turned back to the telephone. 'Mrs. Shore, this is Linda Payne, only it's Linda Gordon now. I was calling to ask Dr. Shore to dinner tomorrow. And you too, of course.'

'Oh, my dear child, I'm so glad to hear from you! I've been so worried about you since your fath — -' She stopped abruptly, then her voice rippled on. 'About dinner. I simply can't tomorrow. But perhaps the doctor can come. I'll tell him to call you. I just know he'd be delighted.'

'Please. Tell him it will be around one o'clock.' She hung up with a deep breath.

'That's all.' Storm gestured back toward the study.

'Those people; you wanted to know where they are?' Linda said slowly.

'And you were shot at just now,' Storm reminded her quietly. 'The person who fired the shot is *not* at home. He's in a car.'

'But they . . . all of the people you called are my friends,' she protested. 'Charles Gabriel's my godfather; he was one of Father's closest friends. I've known Dr. Shore for years; he was even closer to Father than Gabriel. And Glenn is my cousin!'

Storm looked at her with curious intensity. 'Remember what you've said: they were all your friends . . . We'll come back to that later.'

They returned to the study. Walt was inspecting the broken lamp. Storm prowled about the room, pausing at the window and the French doors. Finally he returned to his chair. Walt and Linda sat down, and Storm lit a cigarette. 'We were discussing the woman who purchased the pin from Allegretto,' he said quietly.

'Allegretto had noticed that she seemed the least bit unsteady on her feet, as if she might be faint. He watched her leave and cross the street, and thereafter he saw her again, two or three times, always wearing the pin. And each time he observed that she seemed . . . well, not strong. I thought it likely, if such was the case and she was walking, that she must live in the immediate neighborhood. After a morning of questioning, I located the place — a studio hotel called the Sequin Arms on Ninth Street, two blocks from Allegretto's.' Storm paused a moment, then continued:

'The manager of the Sequin remembered the woman and the pin. The name she had used, he said, was Helen Walker. She had come in ten days before, carrying only a worn mustard-yellow suitcase patched with adhesive tape in places. He knew nothing of her — her business, previous address, nothing. She'd lived very quietly in a small room, having no visitors that he knew of. She had seemed unwell, suffering from a cold. Though her rent was paid through the week, he'd not seen her in several days. I went to her fourth-floor room.'

Storm paused and frowned. 'I was too late. Not one personal item remained in the room. All clothes were gone, all luggage, everything. The windows, the chairs, table, bed, even the walls and bath had been cleaned of fingerprints. Someone had done a perfect job of destroying all clues to the woman's identity. I have a name — Helen Walker, and that's probably a fake. I have no idea who she was.'

'Was?' Linda echoed. 'You think she may be dead?'

'I do.' Storm leaned forward and took a deep breath. 'I found her room on the tenth. On the morning of the eleventh I came here to report to your father. I told him exactly what I'd found, what Allegretto had told me. I told him I did not regard the woman as a pure crackpot. There was plenty that was peculiar about her, certainly, but there was also a vein of deadly seriousness running through the events.' Storm paused and held up his fingers as he enumerated.

'Remember: the woman had lived at the Sequin only ten days, during which time she was known to have stayed close to her room; and she was not known to have had any visitors. She used the name Helen Walker. I checked at Police Headquarters; I was unable to find a wanted or missing person of that name or of that description. I am almost certain the woman moved into the Sequin to hide herself and her contemplated activities. Now,' Storm said pointedly, 'from whom was she trying to hide, and what activities did she wish to hide?'

'The blackmailing of my father,' Linda supplied.

Storm nodded slowly. 'That was the activity she wished to conceal, we'll assume. But did she go into the Sequin on account of your father, to throw him off her trail if he tried to trace her? It hardly seems likely. He knew nothing about her to start with; there is little reason to assume that he would have had a better chance of tracing her to her previous locality. No . . . ' Storm said intently, 'we must assume that she moved

46

into the Sequin under a fake name to hide her blackmail effort from some *other* person, someone who knew her, knew where she lived, how to find her, someone who *opposed* the blackmail. That assumption becomes even more logical when certain other facts are considered.

'For instance, while she displayed some caution in coming to your father and in arranging for the second meeting, it was not nearly the caution of an outright and experienced blackmailer. Also, you will remember that she warned him that he was to tell none of his friends of her visit, even though he notified the police. Twice she warned your father in such a way. So doesn't that suggest strongly that she was trying to hide her blackmail action from some *other* person; and that other person becomes, by the woman's own words, a friend of your father?' Storm paused pointedly. 'And finally, when we remember that your father was impressed with a certain sincerity about the woman, and when we remember that she feared the police less than she feared this other person, we reach the conclusion that the woman was trying to sell your father a genuine warning. She wanted a lot of money, yes; but she did have something to sell. Do you see?'

'Yes . . . Please go on,' Linda said quickly.

'I think the woman feared this other person, and tried to hide from them. I think she realized her game was dangerous, far and apart from police actions. And finally, from the blood on the driveway near her pin, we must conclude that the danger she feared finally overtook her. She was injured there, if not actually murdered. She has not been seen around her room or hotel since then. And all personal belongings and clues to her identity have been removed from her room.'

'So you also think that if you knew who she was, you would be able to learn who this *other* person was?' Linda wondered.

'That is the point,' Storm agreed with a nod. 'An identification of the woman would lead to an identification of her, shall we say, killer. I believe that firmly. Otherwise, why would such pains have been taken to clean the room at the Sequin?' He leaned back and lit another cigarette.

'As I said, your father and I discussed all this, all these probabilities, on the morning of the eleventh. As you know, Mrs. Gordon, your father was a very cautious man. He decided it was foolish simply to ignore everything that had happened. He thought it wise to accept the possibility that something might be threatening you. He decided that, until the matter was cleared up and explained, you should leave here.'

'Oh!' Linda sat up straight. 'Then that's why he insisted that I take my vacation earlier than I'd planned!'

'That's why. So, you remember, you left the house on the morning of the twelfth, Friday. You drove into New York and shopped that day. You didn't notice, but I was following you.'

'You followed me that day?'

Storm smiled faintly as he nodded. 'That evening you met Mr. Gordon for dinner and a show. I sat in the seat behind you at the theater. I was never far from you; I followed you and Mr. Gordon from the theater to your hotel. I stayed in the lobby that night. I trailed you to Newark the next morning, where you took the ten-twelve train for St. Louis. We didn't want you to leave from New York. And that,' he said, 'was a week ago today.' He stopped and looked at her steadily.

'It was noon when I got back to my office. A message was waiting for me from your father; he wanted to see me at once. I came out, arriving here at two that afternoon. Goode took me to your father's bedroom upstairs. He was sitting in the chair at his desk. He was so ill he could hardly move or talk. He — '

'My father was ill!' Linda echoed sharply. 'But he was perfectly well when I left here the day before!'

'He was ill from shock and fear,' Storm explained. 'He told me this: At nine-thirty the evening before, while he was sitting at that same desk writing a letter; he happened to glance up just in time to see a shadow racing, falling across the wall in front of him. It was the shadow of an arm, a hand. He twisted and turned

50

quickly, just in time to glimpse a masked man, and just in time to escape the downward lunge from a knife in the man's hand. The knife missed your father by inches and buried its point in his desk.'

'You mean,' Linda gasped thinly, 'that while I just sat in that theater with Walt . . . a man tried to . . . to murder my father!'

'I mean exactly that,' Storm said quietly. 'Your father seized the lamp from the desk and hurled it wildly at the man. The room was thrown into darkness. Your father tried to reach a gun he kept in his desk. The would-be killer fled.' Storm paused and his voice lowered. 'Your father tried to contact me; I was following you. He spent that entire night awake in his chair, behind the locked door of his room, with the gun in his hand. By the time I arrived, his nerves were shattered; he could scarcely talk. Everything about our meeting was strange,' he recalled slowly.

'What do you mean, strange?' Linda asked.

'It's hard to explain. I mean that there

was something besides his fear, his anxiety over you; there was more than the memory of the attempted murder. There was apathy, almost utter resignation in his face, his speech and manner — a resignation to defeat, it seemed to me. There was no hope or spirit about him. He was like a man already dead in mind, whose body was soon to die. He — '

'Stop! Stop it! I can't stand to — ' Linda cried.

Instantly Walt was beside her.

Storm was silent. His warm brown eyes watched her gravely for a few moments. 'You're ready for me to go on now?' he asked quietly at last.

'Yes, I . . . You must go on. I'm sorry.'

'I went into such detail because of what follows,' he explained. 'Your father told me he was giving Goode a vacation. He himself was going into New York to stay at the Markham Hotel until he could regain control of his nerves and mind, until the motive behind the violence could be understood. He intended to place himself under the care of Dr. Shore; he didn't want to be disturbed for a few days. He promised to call me when he had got hold of himself again. He gave me a check and said it was to cover any services of the future that I might provide; he begged me to stay on this case until it was closed, and to handle it as quietly as possible.

'And finally,' Storm said, leaning forward, 'he told me he'd been thinking about Helen Walker's warning to him not to reveal her visit to any friend of his, even though he notified the police. He told me that he had few friends; that he had grown apart from his business associates since his retirement from his company. He said he could name only four people whom he regarded as close friends. They were Goode, Dr. Clifton Shore, Charles Gabriel, and Glenn Darby. Then he told me he realized that he'd made a stupidly dangerous will involving each and all those people. He said he'd already written Gabriel in regard to changing that will. He assured me that Gabriel was absolutely trustworthy, and that it was only a matter of a day or two until Gabriel would make the suggested changes. He reaffirmed his faith in Gabriel. But,' Storm said with a smile, 'that was why I was interested in the whereabouts of those various people at the time the shot was fired this evening.' He leaned back.

'So, at three o'clock, I left. Your father declined a ride into New York with me; he wanted to write some letters. Goode had gotten him a ticket on the seven-ten train for that evening. I left him seated at his desk; he was staring at a vase of tulips, and his lips were open, as if he was speaking to himself. He looked infinitely tired, hopeless. The next day I learned that he hadn't checked into the Markham. I learned that Shore hadn't heard from him. I got no answer to a call. I came out, found the house locked. I forced my way in and searched. I found your father in his bedroom, stretched across the bed. His pistol was in his hand. There was a bullet in his right temple,' Storm said. 'Later the examiner established that he had been dead between eighteen and twenty-one hours. In other words he had died between four in the afternoon and seven in the evening of the previous day, after I had left him sitting in his bedroom. Suicide, of course, was the assumption.'

Storm stopped and leaned back. He mopped his moist face. 'I know, and you must surely know, Mrs. Gordon, that it was not suicide. Your father was murdered. He *knew* he was going to be murdered when he talked with me that last afternoon. Call it premonition, intuition, anything you like — your father felt death coming. But he was not a man who wanted to die, to kill himself! He was like a man who had struggled and lost — and he knew he had lost.'

'But I don't . . . can't see,' Linda breathed. She tried to think. Her brain refused to function, to grasp the total picture. Even her senses refused to register the full depth of shock. She could only stare mutely at the eyes of the man before her.

'I'm sorry I had to tell you this,' Storm said slowly. 'Everything connected with murder assumes the shape of grotesque fantasy in the minds of sensitive people. But murder has been here once,' he told her bluntly. 'Tonight it tried to come again. You must understand one thing now, Mrs. Gordon: you are in danger. You must be careful.' He stopped, glanced at his watch, rose with an air of finality. 'You're tired. Nothing more can be done now. With your permission, I'll spend the night here. Tomorrow we'll go on. But there is one last thing I should mention,' he added. 'Your father gave me a check in payment for future services. He asked me pointedly to stay on the case, to handle it as quietly as possible. For his reasons, as well as my own, the police have no knowledge of what happened prior to his death. And his death, curiously, was confirmed as suicide; I'll discuss that tomorrow also. But,' he went on, 'you have the right to ask me to withdraw from the case. In that event, I'll place all the information I have in the hands of anyone you choose. I hope, however, that you will wait until tomorrow to make your decision. There are reasons not entirely egotistical,' he said with a dry smile, 'why I feel I'm better prepared than anyone else to handle the case. That, too, I'll explain tomorrow.'

'Yes,' Linda agreed mechanically. Walt rose. 'But there are so many things I don't understand!' she protested. She glanced at her husband. '*You* knew! I heard you when you telephoned Storm and — '

'But it's after midnight now, Linda,' Gordon interrupted patiently. 'You're tired. I'll explain all that tomorrow.' He touched her hand. Reluctantly she rose.

'But I want to know — ' she began stubbornly again.

'I think your husband's right,' Storm said. 'Go to bed. Draw a line in your mind between what happened tonight and what will come tomorrow. You'll see things clearer that way.' He smiled. 'Good night.'

Linda sighed, and gave it up. Slowly she and Walt left the study and climbed the stairs. In the upper hall she paused before the closed door of her father's room. Her fingers touched the knob.

'Not tonight,' Walt said firmly. 'Leave it alone. You'll only torture yourself.' He led her on, into their own bedroom. He snapped on the light, closed and locked the door, then lowered the shades at the windows.

'Walt, please,' Linda spoke suddenly. 'Look at me . . . I've got to know. How much of this have you known all along?'

He turned to face her. 'Some of it, darling,' he said finally. 'Storm questioned me, as I'm sure he questioned the others. That was before your father's death. He alarmed me. I could tell that something was wrong — something concerning you. Then I saw him following us that night we went to the theater, the night before you left New York. That made me even more uneasy and worried; I'd made inquiries before that and learned what his business was. So . . . after you left town the next day, I telephoned him. I suggested that we have dinner together that night. He agreed. By the time we met for dinner, he'd had his last talk with your father. I suppose that by that time he was reasonably convinced I had nothing to do with the affair. He knew we were engaged; he knew I'd been at the theater the night before when the attack had been made on your father. He was willing to tell me a few of the details. You . . . Well, you can imagine my reaction. I thought about you, alone, on your way to New Mexico, not knowing what was happening. At first I was angry with Storm for not telling me, for letting you go. Then I suddenly made my decision that night at dinner.'

'To meet me in New Mexico,' Linda supplied slowly.

Walt nodded. 'I told Storm, explained that we planned to get married in the fall. I told him I wanted to be near you if there was any danger. That night I started calling for a plane reservation. I got one by eight the next morning. I left at eleven that morning, and was waiting for you when you left the train at El Paso, Texas.'

'So you came . . . married me so quickly because you were afraid something might happen to me,' she murmured distantly.

'I married you because I loved you,' he said quietly. 'You know that, Linda.'

'But it . . . The feeling,' she whispered. 'We were married for reasons I didn't even understand — '

'No. You're looking at it the wrong

way,' he said anxiously. 'It was wrong to deceive you, perhaps. I knew your father was dead when we were married. Storm had wired me at El Paso. I didn't tell you because I was afraid you wouldn't go through with it if you knew, and I . . . I had to be with you. Linda! You understand that, don't you?' he asked harshly as she stared at him.

'Understand?' she echoed starkly. 'I don't know . . . don't understand anything tonight,' she whispered. She closed her eyes and clenched her fingers.

'But us — me and you!' he said anxiously. 'You understand that much? You know I love you? Say that much, for God's sake!'

Linda opened her golden-brown eyes. Walt's slender face, his worried black eyes took form before her. Suddenly she opened her arms.

'Oh, I do! I do know that,' she whispered. 'That's all I know tonight.'

4

Linda awoke with a start. Above her was the familiar pattern of the wallpaper. The sun shone through the window, silhouetting the shadows of tree limbs over the distant wall. A medley of sounds reached her ears, sounds reaching back into childhood: the brisk chirping of birds in the field; the thin, sucking whine of speeding tires on the highway; the scraping of a branch as the breeze blew it against the cornice of the house. The odors came back from memory: the scents of evergreen and grass, of sun on the dusty weeds.

In that moment she lived suspended — away from the unremembered present, floating through a pattern of yesterday. Yet floating with a hollowness in her stomach.

'Awake, darling?'

The words shattered the moment. She turned. In the bathroom stood Walt, shaving soap coating his cheeks and chin.

'Better be getting up.' He gestured with his razor. 'I heard Storm moving around an hour ago.

Storm ... The hollowness in her stomach congealed into reality. A tide of recollection swept back about her. Slowly she pushed back the covers and sat up. She stiffened as she saw the small blunt gun on the table by Walt's side of the bed. She pulled her eyes away as he came into the room. He stooped to kiss her, and his cheeks smelled of shaving lotion.

'It's a wonderful day, darling,' he observed. 'I smell coffee.'

'Um-hum.' She looked through the window. Last night was over now ...

'It is a wonderful day,' she agreed cheerfully. 'I'll be dressed in a minute.' She turned toward the dresser. When next she looked, the gun was gone. *I know*, she thought, *why Walt's seldom left me alone since the day he joined me in El Paso.*

She stopped brushing her hair. She closed her eyes and tried to picture the person who had crept to the French door the night before, who had raised a gun to kill her. Some 'friend' of her father?

Goode? Darby? Shore? Gabriel?

At last she shook her head. No face would fit the figure of murder.

It was nine-thirty when they joined John Storm on the sunporch. He rose. He was smoking and his empty dishes were pushed aside.

'After the first half-hour, I quit waiting,' he said with a smile.

'I don't blame you,' Linda said. She looked at him for the first time by daylight. He seemed younger this morning than she had thought last night. It would be hard to guess his age, she thought.

She sat down with Walt as Goode brought the grapefruit. 'I apologize for being stubborn last night,' she said. 'I was tired.'

Storm gestured depreciatively. 'Oh, yes. Dr. Shore called. He'll come to dinner. That leaves Darby, and we don't want him until late afternoon anyway.' He tapped the edge of the table. 'I've had to move rather carefully to avoid any curiosity from the police,' he said slowly. 'I was rather surprised when they accepted your father's death as suicide. I have a feeling that Dr. Shore can tell me a lot about that if — '

'Goode? You know he's in the kitchen there?' Linda said softly. 'Do you want him to hear?'

'He understands. Your father explained to him my position. Goode has been very discreet.' Storm frowned. 'As I was saying, there was something almost too easy about the suicide verdict the police turned in on your father. A murderer seldom frames an acceptable suicide scene. Either the police did a sloppy investigation — which is also doubtful — or they got some solid testimony from someone that made the suicide reasonable. And they got testimony from Shore,' he added pointedly. 'Furthermore, Shore enjoys a certain respect at Headquarters in New York. He was once on the medical staff. His word would carry weight if — ' Storm stopped and leaned to one side. He peered down the driveway that curved from sight around the south corner of the house.

'Gabriel,' he murmured. 'I had hoped

he wouldn't come so early.' Up the drive came a heavy gray sedan. 'By the way,' Storm asked suddenly, 'what do you think of Gabriel?'

'Oh, he's just a gallant old bag of wind,' Linda said lightly. 'You know, of course, he's not my uncle. He's my godfather. I just call him that to please him.'

'I hope,' Storm grunted, 'that he'll condescend to read the will. I haven't been able to do anything with him.'

The sedan stopped at the walk leading from the driveway to the door of the sunporch. The huge florid face of the lawyer framed itself at the window. His glasses were perched on his damp forehead, and his wiry gray hair bristled.

'Hot!' he announced. He opened the door and heaved himself out on the walk. He buttoned his vest, dragged his briefcase from the car, and slammed the door behind him. 'Damned hot!' he reaffirmed. He waddled into the shade of the sunporch and deposited a kiss on Linda's hand. 'Well, good morning, my child.'

'Good morning, Uncle Gabe. You know

Walt. And I believe you have met Mr. Storm.'

'Storm?' He revolved violently and hauled the glasses down from his forehead. 'Storm! Well, you!' he growled. Then he peered back toward Linda. 'I understood you didn't know this man,' he said accusingly.

'I didn't. I mean, I met him only last night.'

Gabriel grunted softly as he eased his bulk down into a chair. He clutched the briefcase in his lap and shot a second glance of bright suspicion in Storm's direction.

'Would you like some coffee, Uncle Gabe? You must have started early and — '

'What have you let this man talk you into?'

'But he . . . Father retained him, Uncle Gabe. He is — '

'Sit down! I know what he is. Investigator, he says. What in God's name do you want with an investigator? Answer me that. I cannot approve of any such — '

'Suppose we ignore your approval or

disapproval,' Storm said abruptly. 'I believe Mrs. Gordon wants to have her father's will read.'

Gabriel jerked as if he'd been struck. 'Now, see here! I — '

'Please, Uncle Gabe,' Linda interrupted quickly. 'There's no reason to be angry. Mr. Storm is right about the will. I'm curious. I'd like you to read it. Now,' she added uneasily.

Gabriel stared at her, then he snorted. 'Very well,' he replied peevishly, 'but I intend to make my position absolutely clear before I begin. In the first place, matters of personal finance aren't to be bandied around on just anybody's say-so. Second, your father and I were old friends. He entrusted me with the administration of his estate, without bond. And I must say your father was a shrewd man. I doubt he would have approved of this sort of thing.'

Gabriel blinked owlishly at Storm, then zipped open the briefcase. Pages of a legal document rustled furiously. 'You wish to hear the entire instrument?' he demanded.

Linda glanced at Storm in confusion.

'Suppose,' said the detective agreeably, 'you simply give us the approximate assets and the manner in which the assets are to be divided.'

'Very well, sir,' Gabriel agreed acidly. His face disappeared behind the pages. 'The estate of Gregory Payne is comprised of this house, the furnishings therein, and the estate adjoining, comprised of nine acres of land. There are other assets, namely: three thousand shares of common stock in the Payne-Eden Tobacco Company, one hundred bonds of the year 1996 in the New York and National Railway, fifty bonds of the year 1972 in the Cornwall Tool and Die Company, and certain government bonds, the value of which at maturity will be one hundred thousand dollars.' Gabriel paused and flipped a page.

'The estate is to be divided as follows: After certain charitable bequests, mentioned in a previous section, seven-eighths of the remainder will go to Linda.' Gabriel lowered the will and pointed at her. 'The remaining one-eighth will be divided in equal parts among four people whom Gregory Payne designated as his close friends: Glenn Hill Darby, Lester Goode, Clifton Shore, and Charles Gabriel. Myself,' he grunted. He lowered the will and glared at Storm. 'That, sir, in loose terms, is the nature of the instrument.'

'What is the approximate total value of the estate, leaving out the part that goes to charity?' Storm asked.

'Something less than a million dollars. A little more than eight hundred thousand, I should say offhand.'

'In other words,' Storm mused, 'about seven hundred thousand for Mrs. Gordon, and the other one hundred thousand in equal parts between you, Shore, Goode, and Darby — making about twenty-five thousand dollars for each of you.'

'Roughly, that's correct. That doesn't take into account the taxes. Mrs. Gordon, in the final analysis, will receive much less in proportion because of the heavier taxes on the larger amount.'

Storm nodded absently. He fingered a cigarette from his pack. 'You haven't overlooked anything important?'

'I have not,' Gabriel snapped.

'You don't mind if I glance through it?' Storm reached across the table and neatly slipped the will from Gabriel's fingers. The man grunted angrily. Linda watched Storm flip the pages, pausing to glance at each. He stopped, frowning.

'Here is something,' he mused slowly. 'It provides that, in case Linda Payne should die without heir or issue, the entire estate, exclusive of charitable bequests, shall then be divided in equal parts between Glenn Darby, Lester Goode, Clifton Shore, and Charles Gabriel.' He lowered the will and looked steadily at Gabriel. 'In other words, he said flatly, 'if Mrs. Gordon had died before her marriage, the entire estate would have been split four ways, giving you, Goode, Darby, and Shore two hundred thousand dollars each upon Payne's death. Two hundred thousand each, instead of the twenty-five thousand,' he mused. 'So . . . Mrs. Gordon's death, before marriage, would have meant a profit of a hundred and seventy-five thousand dollars to each and every person mentioned in that will. Am I right, Gabriel?'

'If you want to put it in brutal terms, yes,' Gabriel snapped. 'However, the clause was entered simply to care for that most improbable eventuality. It is meaningless now. Linda is alive. She is married. Her husband becomes her legal heir, I assume.' He turned to peer at her.

'Oh, yes. Yes, of course,' she agreed quickly.

'The clause is meaningless now,' Storm said slowly, 'unless we go a step further into the almost impossible and consider what would happen if both Mr. and Mrs. Gordon were soon to die. I understand that you have no heirs, Mr. Gordon?'

'No, none. My mother and father are dead. I have no brothers or sisters — no close relatives at all,' Walt said.

Gabriel snorted. 'Linda and her husband look healthy to me.'

'And the difference between twenty-five and two hundred thousand dollars looks healthy to me,' Storm countered. He paused and tapped the table gently. 'Or, suppose someone wasn't aware that

Linda Payne had recently been married . . . ' he said softly, as if thinking aloud.

'What are you driving at, Mr. Storm?' Gabriel demanded bluntly.

'Only thinking,' the detective replied absently. He regarded the will thoughtfully as he folded it and landed it back to Gabriel. 'By the way, how many copies were made of that will?'

'Two. One for my files and one for Gregory Payne.'

'When was that will made?'

'Three months ago, shortly after Gregory Payne suffered a heart attack. He began then to put his affairs in final shape.' Gabriel sneezed and jabbed at his nose with his handkerchief. 'Damned tulips!' he growled. 'Excite my asthma every time.'

Storm tapped the table deliberately. 'Since that time did Payne ever suggest that he might want to change that will?'

Linda's eyes moved from the detective to Gabriel's face. She saw him swallow. His tongue moved over his lower lips.

'I remember nothing like that,' he said.

Linda breathed sharply. Walt tapped her knee beneath the table. Storm leaned back and yawned. 'Just wondering,' he said idly. 'I wonder what Payne did with his copy of the will?'

'I haven't the slightest idea,' Gabriel announced shortly. He fumbled for a cigar. At that moment the door from the kitchen opened and Goode stood there, an expression of mingled discomfort and intensity on his aged gray face.

'Sir, if . . . if I may speak to you, sir,' he stammered to Storm. The detective rose quickly and vanished into the kitchen.

Soon, he returned, glanced at his watch, then at Linda.

'Mrs. Gordon, I'd like you to come with me,' he said suddenly. He looked at Walt and arched his brows in Gabriel's direction. 'Your husband and Mr. Gabriel will excuse us a few minutes. I told Goode that Darby would be over this afternoon.'

'We'll try,' Walt said. 'Have a good time.'

Linda rose. Storm opened the door that led to the walk outside. Linda followed him across the gravel driveway, past the garage, and across the back lawn to the steep decline that fell toward the creek. They passed the low, glass-enclosed hothouse.

'We're not just taking a walk?' she said softly.

He said nothing more as they picked their way carefully down the bank of the ravine and crossed the narrow wooden bridge that spanned the stream. Silently, they climbed the opposite bank and came into a rolling field of weeds and trees, through which twisted a footpath. At last, Storm stopped at a thick clump of trees. A rock bench sat in the shade. He nodded for Linda to sit down, then glanced back in the direction of the house. He sat down beside her.

'Tell me about Glenn Darby,' he said.

Linda glanced at him curiously. 'Well, he's my cousin. My mother and his mother were sisters. I've known him always. His father built that stone house — you can see the roof from here.' She pointed across the field. About three-quarters of a mile away, in a dense growth of trees, rose a massive house of gray stone. The slate roof glinted and gleamed in the bright sunlight. 'His father was quite wealthy. Glenn was about ten when both his parents died of pneumonia. He was the only child. For a while a great-aunt came there to live. A few years later — it was when Glenn was eighteen — she died, and left Glenn alone with two servants. He never has had a normal life. He would go to school for a while, then quit and come back there to stay. After a while the servants drifted away, and Glenn lived in the place entirely by himself. He isn't . . . well, very social. Not anymore.'

'He tells me he's a writer — a dramatist.' Storm looked at her questioningly.

'He's tried to be. That's the only thing he ever really worked at, but . . . ' Linda paused and frowned. 'Glenn's writing is just like he is. Sort of tangled up and complicated. It doesn't make sense very easily. He always writes tragedies, and the plots are always touched with a kind of fantasy. Maybe they're supposed to be symbolic, but I never could understand them.'

'I understand he's had two plays produced on Broadway.'

'Oh, that.' Linda made a hopeless gesture with her hands. 'He produced them himself when everyone else turned them down. They were both terrible flops. That's what ate up such a lot of his money. They were so strange and impossible, they didn't have a chance. Everything he writes is like that. I don't suppose he's ever made a penny from any of his writing.'

Storm studied her a moment. 'You're suggesting that Darby may be unbalanced — is that it?'

Linda hesitated, then nodded slowly. 'I suppose so. He's very emotional — happy one minute and terribly depressed the next. And his drinking — whenever he starts, he can't stop until he's drunk. And it always makes him melancholy and bitter. Then he . . . That's all, I suppose.'

'It might help if you finished what you started to say, Mrs. Gordon,' Storm suggested quietly.

'But the rest is . . . only a pathetic flaw in his nature,' Linda said uncomfortably. 'He has no money now. He wasted a lot on little things. The two plays lost everything he put into them. Then, two years ago, he got mixed up in some trouble with a narcotics ring in New York; that cost a great deal before he got out. You see, he had a fantastic idea that he'd do a novel about the New York underworld; he decided to live in it while he gathered material. He moved down on the lower East Side. In less than three months, he was implicated in a dope charge. Some of his new friends had been using him to deliver heroin. The police learned about it. They raided his room in a small hotel and found heroin concealed there. Glenn hadn't known a thing about what was happening, but it cost a lot to get out of that. Father got Gabriel to help Glenn. Since then, nothing good has happened to him. He's been drinking more. He had to sell the big house. He moved into the servants' house and kept a small piece of the land. But anyway, because of his lack of money, and utter inability to do anything to make any more, he has . . . taken little things.'

'From whom?' Storm asked quietly.

'From us. Father. I've known it. Father knew it. Goode knows. It was a sort of gentlemen's agreement that it wouldn't be recognized. And the things were never much: a bottle of whiskey, a ten-dollar bill, things like that. Finally, Father began leaving a twenty-dollar bill around whenever Glenn came over and drank. Glenn would take it when no one was looking. You see, Father felt sorry for Glenn, and I suppose he knew he couldn't be helped.'

'Why didn't Glenn borrow outright?'

'Because he felt he'd never be able to pay, I suppose. That would have humiliated him. He has a strong, strange pride. This other way . . . well, no one ever knew, we pretended.'

She paused. Storm was regarding her with a frown.

'You have a lot of sympathy for him, don't you?' he mused.

'I . . . Yes.' Linda touched her cheek slowly. 'I suppose once I loved him. When I was young in college and Glenn was different,' she said distantly. 'He'd drive up in his car and take me to dances. He'd write poems. I wasn't popular then. It seemed very romantic. It lasted less than a year, but . . . but somehow Glenn never realized it was over.' She stopped. She drew a deep breath. 'But I am fond of him. And very sorry for him,' she said simply.

'I see.' Storm looked at his cigarette, then flipped it away and rose. 'Let's invite Glenn to come over.'

Linda rose. She started to speak as they turned along the twisting path that led across the field toward Darby's house. Storm spoke first: 'Who knows you're married, Mrs. Gordon?'

'Why, not many people. I told Uncle Gabe yesterday when I saw him; he hadn't read my letter. I wrote Glenn a note from New Mexico. Goode knows, of course. I can't think of anyone . . . Oh, yes. I told Mrs. Shore last night when we telephoned her.'

'But the Shores hadn't known before then?'

'I doubt it. I hadn't written them. And

they don't get along with Gabriel or Glenn.'

'But you did write Darby?' Storm persisted.

'I'm sure. It was the same day I wrote Uncle Gabe.'

'So Dr. Shore, of the four people mentioned in that will, was the only person who didn't know you were married at ten o'clock last night?'

Linda stopped and stared at Storm. 'You're not thinking that Dr. Shore was the one who fired that shot!'

'I might be. Or I might be wondering why Glenn Darby stole your father's copy of the will.'

'He . . . Glenn stole the will?' Linda echoed.

'Three months ago. Goode told me he saw Glenn take it from the table in the study one evening; he told your father. Your father told him to forget it. You might remember the night — it was your birthday, Goode says.'

'Oh — that night! I remember. The Shores were there to dinner. And Walt. But why should Glenn steal a will? It has no value, does it?'

Storm shook his head. 'But Glenn knew, therefore, that your death would profit him. Perhaps Shore saw the will that night and realized the same thing. Gabriel certainly knew. And Goode . . . ' Storm frowned wryly.

'But all those people. They are my — ' Linda protested.

'Your best friends,' Storm supplied. 'But remember the warning of the missing Helen Walker.' He continued to frown. 'Those people . . . But could there be others?' he mused aloud. 'There must have been other servants besides Goode. Perhaps some who simply hoped, blindly, to inherit by some — '

'Oh, there have been other servants, but none of them could be involved in this,' Linda assured. 'There was a nurse; she left us five years ago to live with her invalid mother in California. There was a chauffeur and yard man named Albert. He left three years ago to work in a defense plant in Texas. After that it was difficult to get servants. Father didn't like those that were sent here. He was accustomed to Goode, and . . . well, Father was rather independent. If he couldn't get what he wanted, he'd take nothing at all. So for quite a while now there's been just Goode, and he couldn't be guilty of anything.'

They walked on along the trail.

5

The scars of Darby's house grew clear as they drew nearer. A window pane was cracked and patched with adhesive tape; the paint was peeling from the boards. In a wide circle about the small house, the grass was worn away, leaving the bare, dark earth. At the edge of grass and weeds, rusting tin cans glistened in the sunlight. Two faded sport shirts dangled listlessly from a line.

Linda followed Storm across the expanse of grassless earth to the screen door. The inner wooden door was open.

'Darby? Are you home?'

There was a creaking sound from within. Soft feet padded across the floor. The large blond man appeared in the shadowed doorway. He wore no shirt. His feet were bare, his eyes bloodshot and haggard, his cheeks unshaven. He blinked dully.

'Oh. You,' Glenn said wearily. 'I

. . . Damn! I didn't see you, Linda. Wait a minute.'

He disappeared. The patter of bare feet turned solid. A drawer slammed. There was the splashing of running water. At last he reappeared, a shirt on. He was combing his hair.

'Into the little mansion,' he invited grandly, pushing open the door. Linda entered first. A small brown-and-white terrier dog scurried between her legs and bounded off into the weeds. Storm closed the door.

'Sit down. It's velvet anywhere,' Glenn said with heavy sarcasm. His voice was rough and tired behind its false bravado. Linda smiled at him. She made the smile remain as his haggard eyes met hers.

'What brought you over? And don't say love or money.'

'Oh, we might,' Storm countered. He stood gazing about the littered and dirty room. Linda's eyes followed his. There was a sagging studio couch, roughly spread with a cotton blanket and a soiled sheet. A cheap portable radio sat on a chair near it. On the chair were also matches, a crumpled cigarette pack, and an overflowing ashtray. Stacks of books and magazines ranged along the far wall. In one corner was a breakfast table and two chairs. On the table was a coffee pot, a cup and saucer, and a can of evaporated milk. A rocking chair, its bottom sagging, was stacked with shirts and underwear. And against another wall was the single object that Linda remembered from Glenn's real home. It was his desk, large and massive, of dark polished oak. There was his typewriter. There were stacks of paper, other magazines. There were bundles of theatrical programs — sole rewards of Glenn's two Broadway productions. There was another ashtray and a small metal box.

'Delightful little Shrine of Inspiration, or maybe you don't think so?' Glenn's ironic voice cut through the silence like a knife. Linda felt a flush mount in her cheeks, as if she had been caught window-peeking. Storm said nothing. He lit a cigarette and wandered slowly toward the desk.

'Don't you ever open your mail,

Darby?' he asked casually. He tapped a stack of envelopes with his finger.

'Why should I? They're all bills. They depress me.'

'Not always. You might even get a wedding announcement.' He turned. In his fingers he held a small, pale-blue envelope. 'Like this,' he said gently, looking Darby straight in the eye.

'Who would I know that got married?' Darby countered listlessly.

Storm's face was utterly bland. He tilted his head toward Linda. Darby blinked. He stared at the man, then turned incredulous eyes on Linda.

'Does he know what he's saying?' he whispered.

'Of course. I was married last Tuesday.'

'You . . . were . . . married . . . last . . . Tuesday . . . ' Darby swallowed. Then a deep flush swept up over his face, and into the roots of his blond hair. He choked. 'But you . . . Why in hell didn't you tell me!' he almost shouted. 'Last night! I saw you last night! Why didn't you tell me then?' he demanded furiously.

'But I thought you knew. You saw Walt

there, and I'd written you. And I don't see why you're so — '

'You married Walt? I didn't know you . . . ' His harsh words drained into silence. The tense lines of his face slowly relaxed. A wan smile stretched across his lips. 'But you should tell me those little things, darling. You know I never open letters.'

'I certainly know nothing of the kind,' Linda retorted. 'I — '

'Why should she have told you, Darby?' Storm interrupted softly.

Darby turned jerkily. His lips parted. He swallowed.

'After all, I am her cousin, you know.'

'But was there some other reason?'

'Certainly not. After all, Linda's free, twenty-one, and — '

'Perhaps, had you known of the wedding, you would have modified your actions of last night,' Storm interrupted coldly.

Darby blinked. A thin mist of perspiration broke out across his forehead. 'I don't know what in hell you mean,' he said abruptly.

'Don't you?' Storm's eyes were dancing with flecks of angry blackness. 'Where were you at ten o'clock last night?'

'I was in New York.'

'Doing what? Where?'

Darby stiffened. 'Why in hell should I answer you?' he demanded. He turned toward Linda. 'Where does this guy get the idea that — '

'Oh, you don't *have* to answer anything, Darby,' Storm said easily. 'The first time I met you, I told you who and what I was. I explained that you could talk to me or, eventually, to the police. I think you picked me.' He paused a moment. 'And about last night?'

'I . . . just decided to go somewhere — get away from this god-forsaken hole,' Darby replied at last. 'I went to New York. I had a few drinks, here and there. About ten, I . . . I had a little trouble.'

'What kind of trouble?'

'A fight.' Darby wet his lips. 'I was a little tight, I guess. I was walking along Thirty-Second Street near Fifth Avenue. This man was walking toward me. It was dark along there. Nobody was near. Just as he got to me, he tried to hit me — I don't know why. I pushed him away, then I hit him once. He fell into me and we struggled. I hit him again. He got up and staggered off. That was all. But it was ten o'clock, I know.'

'And no one saw this fight?'

'I don't suppose so. I said it was dark,' he repeated stubbornly.

'You'd never seen the man before? You didn't know him?'

'No.' Darby shook his head. 'But he had black hair,' he said swiftly. 'When I hit him, I nicked his scalp. With my cameo ring. I caught a little scrap of his flesh and a couple of strands of his black hair in the ring. I noticed it this morning. It's here, see?' He moved to the desk and opened the small metal box. Carefully, he lifted out a heavy gold ring. On the face of the ring was mounted a massive onyx stone with a raised cameo figure in gray. Darby held the ring toward Storm. 'See? There's even a little blood there, and the strands of hair and flesh. See?'

Linda saw the detective's lips twitch as he took the ring in his fingers. 'You noticed it this morning?' he mused.

'When I started to wash my hands.'

'And you know the fight took place at exactly ten?'

'Yes. I saw a clock just a minute or so later. I'm sure.' Darby swallowed and lit a cigarette. 'Anyway, what's so damned important about a little fuss like that?'

Storm wrapped the ring inside a handkerchief and dropped it in his pocket. 'The reason it's important, Darby,' he said quietly, 'is because it's a lie.'

Darby stiffened. 'What do you mean?'

'The whole concoction is improbable, and the flesh-and-ring story is almost impossible. You say you had the fight at ten last night. Between that time and this morning, when you say you noticed the flesh and hair on the ring, you had innumerable chances to knock the fragments of hair and flesh off the mounting. For instance, whenever you reached into your pocket. When you undressed last night. The greatest chance was while you slept last night. Almost certainly the ring would have rubbed against the bed covers, pulling away the flesh and hair — they aren't securely fastened.'

'I don't give a damn!' Darby exploded furiously. 'That's the way it was, whether you believe it or not! And if you could find the man, you'd be able to prove it. There ought to be some test — compare his blood to the blood on that ring. His hair. He'd tell you it was true about the fight. If you could find him.'

'Out of seven million or more people,' Storm countered acidly. 'And all you know is that he has black hair.' He laughed shortly. 'How about the bar where you had the drinks? Would the bartender remember you?'

'I . . . don't remember the bar,' Darby said haltingly. To Linda he looked like an animal, trapped and hurt. 'I just don't remember,' he repeated emptily. 'And I don't have to take this pushing around,' he added.

Storm started to answer. Suddenly Linda saw his eyes widen. He was looking beyond Darby, across the room and out through the screen door. She saw him blink, and a sharp light flickered into his eyes. He began to cross the room, moving swiftly. He opened the door and let it close silently behind him.

Something in his stealthy intensity moved Linda to follow. She crossed the room to the door. Darby approached the door also. She saw Storm crossing the patch of bare earth. He was bending low, holding out one hand. Softly, he was speaking:

'Doggie . . . Nice, nice doggie . . . '

And in the grass at the edge of the clearing the little terrier beat its tail upon the ground and crawled in pleasure. Storm bent over quickly. Linda saw him pick up a limp, dark object. He glanced at it a moment, then thrust it into his pocket before he turned.

'Oh . . . Oh, my dear God!' Darby breathed beside Linda. The stark empty horror of the whispered words made Linda jump. She turned. His face was gray and bloodless. His eyes were wide and wild and sick.

'Mrs. Gordon,' Storm called briskly. 'We've got to be going.' Linda pushed open the door and stepped outside. She hesitated, then followed Storm as he moved along the trail.

'You asked him over this afternoon?' he whispered.

'You don't think he'd come — not after that?' she gasped.

'Certainly he'll come. Go back and ask him. Tell him . . . ' He glanced at his watch. It was twelve-thirty. 'Tell him three o'clock,' he said.

Linda returned to the little house.

A minute later, she rejoined Storm. She had to trot to keep up with him.

'That dog — what did it have?' she asked breathlessly.

Storm's hand went into his pocket. It came out with a damp and dirt-caked shoe. A woman's black leather shoe: simple, sturdy, low-heeled. 'That,' he said simply.

'But . . . I don't see what that — ' she started.

'Look at it. Hardly worn,' he said, half-impatiently. 'It was not a worthless shoe. It was a good shoe. Look again — see the rot beginning. Feel it — damp all the way through. Think! Think!'

Linda frowned at the shoe, then at Storm. 'I don't see.'

'You will soon. Hurry.'

Now Linda was almost running. They reached the dense clump of trees near the stream. Storm grasped her hand and turned her from the path. They cut across the field, angling back in the general direction of Glenn's house, but in a line that would throw them behind it by about a quarter of a mile.

'Keep your head low,' Storm ordered tersely. 'Darby saw me take that shoe, didn't he?'

'Yes, he . . . He said something. 'Oh, my dear God,' I think it was. He was like a dead man — his face,' she panted.

Storm grunted. 'Here.' He stopped in a dry gully that twisted down toward the creek. He knelt, pulling her down beside him. From where they crouched, Linda could see Darby's house. Storm was watching it with shining, narrowed eyes.

'What are we doing — waiting for?' she whispered.

'To see if Darby's a fool,' he said softly. 'If he . . . ' His words vanished. His hard

94

fingers bit into her arm. 'There!'

And Linda saw. Darby was leaving his house by the rear door. He stopped and looked down in the direction of Linda's house. He stood motionless for perhaps half a minute, then began moving quickly. He hurried across the field, heading toward Storm and Linda, but off at an angle. He kept his head low. From time to time he was lost to sight in gullies, then reappeared.

'Down to the creek where it curves into his land, that's where he's going,' Linda said swiftly.

'Just sit still. Don't move!'

She watched Darby disappear entirely from sight. Then, after perhaps three minutes, Darby reappeared. He was hurrying back toward his house. He passed out of sight again, and Linda heard the slamming of the distant door.

Carefully, Storm rose until he was in a half-standing position. He gestured Linda to do likewise. He continued to grip her arm as he followed the path of the gully until it reached the creek. There he moved along the steep slope of the bank until he gained a place within fifty feet of the point where Glenn Darby had vanished. He crawled up the bank and, bending low, ran across the field and ducked into a dense clump of trees. Linda drew a deep breath and followed. She joined him. He was peering intently about him.

'What's all this?' he asked. He pointed to a pile of rocks.

'This is where an old farmhouse used to be, before Glenn's father bought this land. The house was torn down or burned. Glenn's father made a barbecue pit over there, using the rocks that had been in the foundation of the house. Those used to be benches. We used to have picnics down here years and years ago. And that . . . ' She pointed to a rock- and dirt-filled depression where Storm was looking. ' . . . that used to be the well for the farmhouse. Glenn's father had it filled in years ago, and — '

She stopped. Storm was not listening. He was approaching the round depres- sion, studying the ground nearby. He whistled gently. He straightened to peer toward Glenn's house, then quickly peeled off his coat and rolled up his sleeves. He bent over and rolled a huge rock away. He rolled another away. Linda moved closer. She saw his face — furiously intense. He worked fast. She asked no questions. Rock after rock he hauled from the depression. Swiftly, he scooped out the earth with his cupped hands. Deeper went the hole.

Suddenly, he stopped. He grunted harshly. Linda frowned. She moved forward another step to peer over his shoulder. He turned quickly.

'I don't think I would, Mrs. Gordon,' he said quietly. 'It's not a pretty — ' His words came too late.

Linda's eyes saw only the arm — bony and very white, yet caked in spots with the black, damp soil. The arm of a woman, probably; half-revealed in the depths of the hole!

Linda felt a cold, stabbing nausea hit her stomach and race into her throat. She stumbled backward one step. She felt a scream start behind her lips. Instantly, Storm's hard arm closed over her mouth.

'Don't! *Please* . . . ' he said. She felt him turning her, leading her away. His arm left her mouth. She swallowed thickly.

'It . . . Oh, God, it . . . ' she breathed starkly.

'I know. Now listen,' he said in flat, swift words. 'Go back to your house. Keep down behind the creek bank until you reach the bridge. Then go on in as though nothing had happened — nothing, understand? If anyone asks you, I left you at the bridge. You know nothing about this place or . . . that,' he said, with a tilt of his head. And then he pulled a card from his pocket. 'Call this number in New York. Ask for James Reddy. He's my assistant. Tell him to get out here immediately with the equipment. He'll know what you mean. And tell him to bring the camera. Remember that. When you've done that, join the others, and *try* to act as if . . . Do the best you can; and tell no one what you've seen.' He patted her shoulder and smiled slightly. 'Make it good.'

Linda swallowed. 'But that . . . is she

the — ?' she whispered.

Storm nodded. 'She is. The missing Helen Walker. Now go on.'

Linda fought down her revulsion. She tried to empty her lungs, to fill them with new, clean air. But nothing removed the image burning in her memory — the thin and death-white arm in the damp, rocky hole.

6

Linda crossed the narrow bridge, climbed the steep slope, hurried across the back lawn to the sunporch. As she entered the house, Goode met her.

'I beg pardon, Miss, but it's after one. Dr. Shore is here, and the dinner is — '

'Oh. Yes, of course. We'll eat now. Mr. Storm won't be in for a while,' she said quickly. She hurried on into the hall and toward the front of the house. As she lifted the telephone, she heard Gabriel's voice booming from the half-open door of the study:

'To my mind the most important thing is this: Get the professors out of Washington! Get business back in the hands of businessmen! And as far as taxes go — '

She called the New York number that was on the card. Presently a bland voice answered.

'Mr. James Reddy?' she asked quickly. The voice grunted affirmation. 'This is

Linda Payne, or Gordon. You know who I am?'

'Yes indeed. What is it?' The voice was suddenly alert.

'Mr. Storm asked me to call you. He wants you to come out here immediately. He said to bring the equipment — that you'd know what he meant. And he said to bring the camera.'

'Yes. Is that all?'

'That's all.'

'I'll be right out.' The line clicked. Linda put back the receiver, drew a deep breath. She fixed a smile on her lips as she moved towards the study. When she entered, Gabriel was planted in the center of the rug, a cigar in his mouth as he continued his lecture on the state of the nation. Walt was sitting on the couch, watching the lawyer with a faint smile of amusement. And from a deep chair Dr. Clifton Shore rose and straightened his gaunt, tall body.

'Ah, my dear child. My very best wishes on the surprising news,' he said softly. His voice was deep and lazy. He kissed her gently.

'Thank you, Dr. Shore.' She smiled at him, and her smile was direct and warm. There was something ageless and utterly comfortable about this man. Linda could not remember when he had not been exactly as he was now. Always his hair had been short-cropped and metal-gray, his suit dark blue and dangling from his bony body. His face had always been etched with deep brown lines whose effect was one of half-Lincolnesque power and attraction. Where Gabriel was loud and gusty, this man was quiet and soft-spoken, albeit his words were sometimes touched with acid. Linda felt a wave of welcome serenity flow through her, a quiet calm that drew its strength from the gaunt, homely man before her. 'I'm very glad you came,' she said quietly.

Walt rose and started across the room, a puzzled frown on his face. At that moment Goode appeared at the doorway.

'Dinner is served,' he announced.

'Storm? Where is he?' Walt asked Linda softly.

'He . . . left me at the bridge. He'll be in after a — '

'He left you alone?' Walt exploded in a savage whisper. 'I — '

'Well, let's eat! Nothing like food to take your mind off your troubles,' Gabriel rumbled contentedly. Linda sighed gratefully as they crossed the hall to the dining room. She wanted time to sit down, to think and try to understand.

Absently, Linda watched Goode as he served dinner, but she scarcely heard the desultory conversation during the meal.

'Well, Goode still knows a thing or two about cooking,' Gabriel announced comfortably, pushing aside his plate. He felt into his pockets. 'No cigars,' he grunted. He took a cigarette from the box on the table, and lit it. He peered at Linda. 'Now, I'd just like you to tell me,' he growled, 'what in hell that man Storm is doing around here. Asking personal questions! Prying into your financial affairs!'

'But . . . I thought I told you, Uncle Gabe. Father retained him. Father paid him before . . . ' The words slipped from her lips as she saw Dr. Shore gazing intently at her with his melancholy eyes.

'John Storm is here now?' His question was scarcely a whisper.

'Yes . . . he's out just now, but — ' Linda began uneasily.

'Did he advise you to invite me to dinner?' Again Shore's words were whispered, and his eyes were glowing darkly.

'Why, you know I wanted to see you, and — '

Clifton Shore smiled wearily. 'I'm far too old to be lied to, my dear,' he said patiently. He shrugged his bony shoulders. 'I really should have surmised . . . '

Walt ceased stirring his coffee and looked at Shore. Gabriel did likewise. A brittle, strained silence filled the room. And Linda kept watching the doctor's bottomless, burning eyes.

The still-sultry heat of midday had something to do with the spell on them all; that and the listless drone of the ancient ceiling fan above. As the blades turned, they flicked arcs of shadow through the eyes of Shore, and time seemed to vanish.

'Well? Well, what's the matter with everybody?' Gabriel's gusty voice was like the sudden explosion of a gun. Linda jumped slightly. Walt's cup rattled on the saucer. 'What's the matter here?' the lawyer fumed heavily. 'You, Shore? Do you know him?' He glared at the doctor. 'Damn it, something's wrong around here!'

Shore turned slowly to face Gabriel and Linda, a cloud of quiet contempt gathering in his eyes.

'It never ceases to amaze me,' he said quietly.

'What amazes you?' Gabriel demanded.

'The steamroller of your perception,' Shore said with acid fury. 'Yes, I happen to know this man John Storm. I happen to know that he has written two books on criminal psychology, and that he is regarded as one of the best investigators in this country.'

'Well?' Gabriel blinked. 'I don't care what he is. And what is so slow about my perceptive powers, may I ask?'

'The agile manner in which you concluded that something might possibly be wrong here,' Shore snapped. 'As a prophet, Gabriel, you are a sensational historian. I — '

'Dear me,' an ironic voice interrupted from the hall door. 'So you're still baiting old Gabriel, are you?'

Everyone turned. The speaker was Glenn Darby. Now he was shaved. His hands were thrust into the pockets of his red plaid coat, and his smile was meant to be insolent, but wasn't. His bloodshot eyes roamed away from Linda.

'Now, see here, you degenerate young pup!' Gabriel roared.

'Uncle Gabe! Glenn! Please, all of you,' Linda begged. At that moment the silvery chime of the front door sounded. She remembered the call to James Reddy. Quickly, she rose. 'I'll answer,' she said. 'We might as well go in the study.'

She hurried from the room and to the front door. When she opened it, a short, plump man of about forty stood there, his baby-blue eyes shining brightly, and his bald head glistening in the sunlight.

'Mrs. Gordon? I'm James Reddy,' he said.

'Yes, come in. Mr. Storm is not in right — '

'He is now.' The detective rounded the

corner of the house. 'Hello, Red. Where are the others?' he asked Linda.

She glanced back down the hall. 'In the study now. Everyone's in a bad humor.'

'Not nearly as bad as they're going to be,' he said drily. 'Let's get upstairs in a quiet room a minute.' He entered the hall and moved silently past the closed study door to the stairs. Linda and Reddy followed. They went upstairs and Storm led the way into the northeast bedroom at the rear of the house. He closed the door quickly.

'You brought the equipment?' he asked Reddy swiftly. The man nodded. Storm moved to the east windows and gestured to Reddy. The man joined him. 'You can't see from here because of the trees on this estate, but across there,' Storm said, pointing, 'you'll find another clump of trees and some stones and concrete. You'll find a hole. You'll find the body of Helen Walker.'

Reddy sucked in a quick breath.

'Get over there and get some pictures,' Storm ordered. 'Get her fingerprints. Get everything you'll need now, because we'll have to let the police in on it. We'll arrange our story when you get back. And, Reddy, take a careful look at her left side along the ribs. See if you understand what happened there; take a picture of it.'

'Her left ribs?' Reddy cocked a brow. 'What about them?'

'I don't understand it. The flesh all across the left ribs is covered with long, crisscrossing cuts — like a meshwork of cat-claw scratches. They're not deep. In fact, they hardly broke through the skin. They wouldn't have done any real injury. I just can't understand why they're there at all.' He paused, frowning. 'Get everything and get back here.'

Reddy nodded and departed. Storm turned to face Linda. 'I'd like to ask you a rather intimate question, Mrs. Gordon.'

'What is it?' Linda asked uncertainly.

'It's the usual thing, isn't it, for women to wear a brassiere when they go out — when they're normally dressed otherwise?'

'Usually, yes. I suppose you'd say it depends on their figures. Some women don't wear them, but most do.'

'And don't most women usually wear

slips when they go out?'

'Of course.' Linda looked at him peculiarly. 'But why?'

'There is neither a slip nor a brassiere on the body of Helen Walker. There is a worn black dress which buttons up the front from the waist to the throat. The buttons are spaced about four inches apart, which would have allowed some gaps between buttons. Wouldn't you think, in that case, that she would have been wearing some undergarment between the dress and her body?'

'I'd hope so,' Linda said with a faint smile.

'But she wasn't. I noticed the buttons in the beginning because they'd been buttoned wrong. The lowest buttonhole had been skipped, throwing all those above it out of place. Don't you think a woman would have noticed her error and rebuttoned the dress before going out?'

'I'm sure she would, when the buttons were at the front.'

Storm nodded. 'And then I found the scars — the light cuts I mentioned to Red. They cover an area of about four inches from back to front, and about five inches up and down. There was no bandage on them. They had bled, forming a rectangle of bloodstained flesh. And yet,' he said pointedly, 'the inner side of her dress was scarcely stained at all.' He looked at Linda curiously. 'Can you suggest any explanation?'

'No. I don't see how, if she was wearing the dress,' Linda said slowly. 'The dress wasn't cut?'

'No. That means that someone lowered her dress to inflict the superficial wounds, then buttoned it again — and missed a button in his haste. But *why* did he inflict twenty-five or thirty scratches? Not to kill her — a blow on the head did that. And why,' Storm said softly, 'did this person, at the time he lowered her dress, also remove her brassiere and slip?'

'Oh,' Linda said suddenly, 'don't you see? He had to remove the brassiere to make the cuts. It would have been in the way. And the slip, too, would have been in the way.'

'I see that,' Storm agreed, 'but couldn't he simply have broken the straps of the slip and brassiere and pulled them down, as he did the dress? Why did he remove the slip completely? The brassiere might have been pulled off more easily, but the slip was more of a job. I see no reason . . . '

'No,' Linda agreed slowly. 'Did you find anything that told you who she really was?'

'Nothing. Her purse wasn't there. She wore no jewelry. She had no hat, and her dress looks cheap; it has no identification on it. There was nothing in her pockets but these.' He thrust his hand into his pocket and pulled out a small packet of tissues, neatly folded together. 'Just plain cleansing tissues, such as women sometimes use instead of handkerchiefs. And Helen Walker had a cold, you remember.'

'I was just wondering,' Linda said suddenly. 'Do you suppose there were laundry marks on the slip and brassiere?'

'I thought of that, but don't women in modest circumstances usually wash their own underwear?'

'Many women do. I do. I suppose she would have, of course.'

'The other thing that keeps puzzling me is the bloodstain on the inside of her dress,' Storm said, thinking aloud. 'If the scratches were made very long before she was killed, there would have been more stains on the inner side of the dress — even granted the improbability that she would have gone on her way without applying some bandage to save her dress. But there was almost no stain on the inner side of the dress. That suggests that the scratches were inflicted after she was murdered; in which case she was probably thrown in the hole and her dress did not fall against the bloodstained skin. But even that falls apart,' he said in annoyance, 'because the scratches had been treated, I'm almost certain. I found slight patches of uninjured flesh between the crisscross of scars, and there was a faint red or pinkish color, as if some antiseptic had been applied. The red didn't show amidst the blood.'

'But if the scratches were treated, why weren't they bandaged?'

'I wish I knew,' Storm said bleakly. 'But at least we've got the body. And we know that Glenn Darby has been aware of the grave.'

Linda swallowed. 'Do you think he could . . . have done it?' she asked softly.

'Well, if he didn't, he knows who did, very likely. And I think it's quite possible that he did kill her.'

'Just because he knew where the grave was?' Linda wondered.

'Because of that. Because he needs money, and I feel sure that the same person killed Helen Walker and your father; your father's death meant money to Darby, and he knew it. And also, life seems to come fairly cheap to him.'

'What do you mean?' Linda whispered.

'I slipped up to his house when I left the grave. I was looking through a window when he called in his dog. He had a wire, coiled and ready. He looped it about the dog's neck. He strangled the dog to death, less than an hour ago.'

'He . . . Oh, no!' Linda gasped starkly. 'But . . . but why?'

'To keep the dog from leading us to the grave. That's where the dog got that shoe — he burrowed down and pulled it off

Helen Walker's foot. Darby slipped to the grave and covered the dog's hole, then murdered the dog to prevent his returning.'

'Oh!' Linda touched her throat. 'But to think . . . of Glenn . . . ' she whispered.

'And finally, the flesh and the hair and the blood on his cameo ring,' Storm said softly. 'The concoction of where he was at ten last night! And yet,' he said uneasily, 'why would a sane man resort to such an incredible story unless . . . unless there was a reason?' He frowned. 'Why did Darby spin such an incredible yarn unless . . . unless it is true after all? Darby is no complete fool.'

Storm paced the room. Linda watched him silently.

'No. It wasn't the laundry marks,' he muttered flatly at last. 'Either she never wore a brassiere and slip, or the two garments carried some revealing evidence. Evidence of what . . . ? How . . . ?' He snapped his fingers impatiently. 'If the slip and brassiere she wore at the time of her death carried some evidence of something, then did all her other slips and brassieres carry the same evidence? Were they disposed of? If . . . ' He stopped and stared at the wall, a gleam breaking into his eyes. He snapped his fingers. 'It might be just enough! Just enough!' He hurried into the hall. Linda heard the clicking of the telephone dial.

'Miss Elsie Warner at Hatterman 7-8858,' Storm said. There was a pause. 'Elsie . . . ? Yes . . . I'm afraid I've got some legwork. I want you to try to locate a suitcase: it's been patched by adhesive tape; it's mustard-yellow and worn. I think it might have been checked or put in a locker box, probably in one of the bigger places, and in a locker box where the person who left it would not have been seen. It was put in between the fifth and tenth of this month, and probably has not been claimed. If you can find such a suitcase, unclaimed, try this story on the attendant who is holding it . . . Tell him it belongs to your sister who had to leave town hurriedly, who lost the check or key. Tell him you can describe the contents without seeing them. No . . . they will probably be scented with lilac perfume.

The shoes will be size seven, probably low-heeled and sturdy. The clothes will be inexpensive, designed for a woman in her forties. And there is a chance that there will be no slips or brassieres in the suitcase . . . That's right. Sign any kind of receipt they offer you. Get that suitcase . . . Yes, the bigger places are the best bet. Call me out here at once. Yes, I think so, but, there may be one chance in a thousand. It's worth a try . . . Goodbye.' The telephone clanked down and Storm returned to the room.

Linda was standing at the north window, watching a mountain of purple-black clouds pile up beyond the distant hills. The bright sunlight had vanished. Across the field outside, not a leaf or blade of grass moved. A sticky listlessness filled the stagnant air.

'It'll rain before long,' she said absently as she turned toward Storm. He nodded as he closed the door.

'You'll remember that last night I asked you to wait until today before making your decision about me — whether I'd handle the case. I wanted to explain why

116

I . . . ' His words trailed into an abrupt silence. Facing him, Linda saw his eyes widen in surprise. He was looking beyond her, out through the window.

'Damn! That . . . That's a fire!' He exploded. He plunged across the room to the east window. Linda turned. 'My God! It's Darby's house!' Storm raged. And Linda saw . . .

Through the foliage of the trees in the back garden, a distant blur of crimson flickered and danced. Into the gray, sullen sky, a pillar of black smoke slowly rose, mushroomed listlessly; hung in utter stillness in the stagnant air. And, very faintly, Linda heard the bite and crackle of the distant flames on wood.

'Damn!' Storm exploded furiously again. He turned and plunged across the room, jerked open the hill door, and vanished. She heard his feet thundering down the stairs. She turned and followed quickly. As she reached the lower hall, she heard the back door slamming. The study door opened and Walt looked out.

'What was that? Sounded like some-body — '

'It's Glenn's house! It's on fire!' Linda explained.

Walt blinked. Then he hurried after her as she ran down the hall.

7

Upstairs, a door slammed, and Gabriel's shaggy head appeared over the railing. 'Fire? What the . . . Wait for me!' he roared as Linda and Walt hurried on. His steps pounded down the stairs.

They crossed the sunporch and cut across the back lawn to the path that led to the bridge. As Linda slipped and stumbled down the steep decline of the ravine, she could see only the pillar of lazy smoke hanging in the dirty sky. She heard Gabriel panting behind her. On climbing up the opposite slope, she saw clearly for the first time the fire, a mass of angry crimson flames weaving their hungry pattern at the base of the black smoke. And she now heard the furious rustle of the burning wood.

She saw John Storm. He was standing, motionless, at the fringe of the fire, his hands in his pockets. The reflection of the flames danced over the hard, angry features of his face.

With a muted, low roar, the roof of the cottage crashed in, sending a shower of embers floating upward into the smoke. A minute later, Linda and Walt reached Storm. He gave no indication that he saw them. His eyes stared into the heart of the flames, and a silent fury stained his face.

Gabriel came puffing up. He mopped his sweating face laboriously. 'Well! Not much left there,' he observed breathlessly. 'Probably doesn't have a cent of insurance, either,' he added complacently.

'We forgot to call the fire department!' Linda realized.

'No need for that,' Storm snapped. Linda started at the angry edge to his words. And suddenly she realized that he didn't want the fire department. She glanced toward the lane a quarter of a mile away. It was seldom used; the chances were no motorist would pass and give a warning. She remembered that the owners of Glenn's former home spent most of their time in New York. She listened to the silence above the crackling flames. She found her ears waiting for the wail of a siren. For some reason it seemed cruel to stand and watch the house burn, yet she realized there was nothing that could be done now.

'You didn't see Reddy when you left the house?' Storm asked her suddenly.

Linda shook her head. Unthinking, she glanced across the field toward the clump of trees that concealed Helen Walker's grave. She saw no sign of Reddy. She glanced back to Storm. His eyes, too, were roaming anxiously about the fields.

'Wonder where Shore and Darby are,' Walt said, looking back down the path. 'I don't want the job of telling him.'

'No.' Linda looked back toward Storm as she heard him moving. He was wandering slowly off toward what had been the back of the house. There, in the edge of the tall weeds and grass, he stopped. Linda saw him bend down, as if to tie his shoe. He straightened, turned, and looked in the direction of the clump of trees near the grave. At last he shrugged and started back toward them.

'Guess we'll never know what caused it,' Gabriel said heavily.

Again, Storm glanced at him obliquely. 'We might,' he said tersely. Linda's eyes returned to the mass of smoking ruins. The flames had withered now. Here and there a slender tongue of red licked upward, then subsided. The smoke was turning thin and gray, and as it stirred she saw the iron framework of Glenn's studio couch in the ruins — like a blackened skeleton, twisted and stiff. She saw the metal mass that once had been Glenn's typewriter. She swallowed. The typewriter, ruined and useless, seemed the epitome of Glenn Darby's entire life.

At that moment a thin shred of lightning pierced the mountain of purple-black clouds. Thunder reverberated lazily in the distance. A cool, swift breeze touched Linda's cheeks, and then the first spatter of rain whispered on the grass.

'We better be getting back,' Storm said abruptly. He gestured down the path. As Linda turned, another flash of lightning blazed out of the clouds, illuminating their depths of purple and of blue. Now the wind came gushing across the field. The thunder rocked the earth. The grass shimmered as the patter of rain suddenly broke into an abrupt downpour.

Linda bent her head. Behind her, Walt cursed softly. Gabriel panted heavily. The bank of clouds came rolling in overhead. For about a minute, the world was tinted with a veil of sinister blueness as darkness closed in. Then the darkness congealed, pouring over the half-light, blotting it into blackness.

Ahead of Linda, the figure of Storm grew shadowy and indistinct. The trees blurred. A blinding sheet of blue-white lightning splashed across the sky. For an instant every twig and blade of grass was etched in brilliant relief. The thunder slammed down from overhead. The moment of light was snatched away. The rain became a deep and drumming roar.

No one spoke. Faster, they moved, stumbling along the rough path. They slipped and slid down the ravine, crossed the narrow bridge, and struggled up the opposite bank. As they reached the crest, the light from the kitchen window shone through the darkness. Goode's anxious face looked out.

They reached the shelter of the sunporch. Linda leaned against the wall to catch her breath. Walt knocked the water from his suit.

'Catch pneumonia!' Gabriel panted heavily. 'Got to get this wet coat off . . . take a hot shower and — '

'Nobody's taking anything right now,' Storm snapped. 'Get in the study. Goode!' he called. The man hustled out of the kitchen. 'Make some coffee. Have you seen a short, plump man around here?'

'No, sir. No one but the lady.'

'What lady?'

'The young lady that wished to speak to Mr. Darby, sir. I don't believe she gave her name. I think you'll find them in the living room, sir.'

Storm turned on his heel and strode into the hall.

'Damn that man!' Gabriel exploded. 'I will not be ordered — '

'You'd better get in the study,' Walt advised flatly. 'Come on, Linda.' He grasped her hand and turned into the hall.

'I'm coming, Walt! Don't jerk so — ' she began.

'Hush!' Storm's tense, low whisper rasped out of the shadowy hall ahead of her. She and Walt stumbled to a stop. Storm was standing perfectly still at the closed door into the living room. Linda swallowed drily. One step . . . two steps forward she tiptoed. Walt's restraining hand stopped her. There she stood, unbreathing, listening. And beyond the steady drumming of the rain outside, she heard a swift voice speaking frantically:

' . . . got to wake up! Glenn, please! Wake up!' the voice begged wildly. The words came from beyond the closed door of the living room. There was a low groan and a grunt.

'Uh . . . huh?' Glenn's voice groaned thickly. 'What you want?'

'Glenn, please! Wake up and listen! I've got to get out of here before someone comes! Open your eyes, Glenn!'

'Who . . . Karen! What in hell — '

'Please — let me talk! Listen! It's about last night! I heard Coke calling somebody this morning — telling him not to leave — '

'Damned wet clothes! Don't know why

I went over there!' Gabriel roared angrily as he bulled his way into the hall and bumped into Walt, who grunted sharply. Instantly, the girl's words ceased. Storm cursed quietly. He straightened and opened the living-room door. Linda heard a stifled gasp from the girl.

'Hello,' Linda heard Storm say. 'I don't think we've met. I'm John Storm.'

There was no answer. Linda moved slowly toward the open door. She saw the girl standing still and stiff in the distant corner. Her hand was across her lips. Her large and beautifully dark eyes were aflame with fright, and her tall, thin body pressed against the wall.

In a chair beside her, Glenn Darby raised dull eyes to stare at Storm. It took perhaps ten seconds for recognition to awake. His fingers gripped the chair arms and he struggled to stand.

Linda saw that he was drunk, his face striving desperately to assemble itself. He shook his head roughly. The dullness faded from his eyes, leaving them glassy and bloodshot.

'We're getting a full house,' he said

thickly. 'Lots of people . . . nice people. Meet Karen. Sweet little damn fool Karen.' He laughed jerkily. 'Nice people. Meet 'em. They hate me, but they're all nice people.'

'I'm glad to meet you, Karen,' Storm said easily. 'Suppose we go in the study.'

'I must go! I . . . I have a taxi waiting . . . ' Her frantic dark eyes fled about the walls of the large room.

'I'm afraid it's too wet,' Storm said firmly. 'And I've already dismissed your cab,' he lied. 'We can call another when the storm stops.' The girl drew herself backward as Storm reached out to take her hand. 'Please,' he said gently. 'I'm not that bad. Come on, Darby.'

'They're not bad,' Glenn said heavily. 'Don't be afraid of the nice man.'

Storm turned and led the girl across the room, past Linda and Walt, into the study across the hall. Darby steadied himself as he rose and stumbled after them. Gabriel prowled into the study after him, his eyes bright with curiosity. Walt and Linda followed.

Storm moved to the windows and drew

the drapes shut. He looked at his watch and scowled. He glanced at the people, then crossed the room. 'Keep them in here a minute,' he said to Walt. He left the room, closing the door behind him. His footsteps faded down the hall.

Linda found herself staring at the girl with a strange fascination. Her eyes, with their dark and restless beauty, dominated her face. Her skin was olive, her hair jet-black and long. Beneath her thin wet coat, she wore a starkly simple dress of flame-red. Her body was slender, even thin to the point of emaciation, as were her fingers and throat. It was only in her eyes that there was vibrant beauty. The rest of her, her body and the taut silence of her, seemed to hold a quality of explosive tension. It was in her rigid silence; it was in the swift throbbing of her throat; it was in the strangely wistful hunger that marked her face. Never had Linda seen anyone remotely like her.

And as she watched, she saw the girl's eyes intent on Glenn's face. In mute eloquence they were speaking to him. Darby sighed and shrugged. Linda heard him curse quietly. She saw a film of tears edge into the girl's eyes. Quickly, she blinked them away, and touched Glenn's arm.

'Please . . . Please,' she whispered. Linda looked away. There was something in the motion too intimate and pathetic to be seen. And as Linda turned, she met Walt's puzzled dark eyes. He, too, had been watching the girl.

'Well, what're we waiting for now?' Gabriel demanded abruptly. 'I'm damned if I get the hang of what goes — '

The door opened and Storm walked in. Behind him came a sleepy-eyed Clifton Shore. Behind Shore came James Reddy, his face flushed. His clothes were disheveled. A faint crimson welt led from each corner of his mouth and across his cheeks. He was holding a towel to the back of his head. His eyes were stony and furious as they swept over the occupants of the room. Goode came last.

'Make some sandwiches and coffee. Bring it in here,' Storm told him. Goode nodded anxiously and vanished. Storm closed the door and surveyed the waiting people. 'Sit down,' he said abruptly.

Linda sat down beside Walt on the small couch. Shore and Gabriel sat down, and Gabriel pulled off his wet shoes. Darby sagged down in a chair apart from the others. Storm maneuvered Karen into a chair at the side of the small desk. He sat down behind the desk, and Reddy leaned against the wall. He continued to dab at the back of his head with the towel as he maintained a stony silence.

'What time was dinner finished, Mrs. Gordon?' Storm asked.

'Just before you came. Just as Mr. Reddy arrived.'

'That was two-thirty exactly. At that time, you and I and Red went upstairs. Reddy came down at about two-forty. We came down about an hour later — at three-forty.' He looked deliberately around the room. 'Where did everyone go after dinner? Shore?'

'I came into this study with Mr. Gordon and Gabriel. I was here less than five minutes, I imagine. I went upstairs, took an aspirin, and stretched out in the front guest room for a nap. I was there when you found me just now.'

'Sleeping very soundly,' Storm added with a hint of sarcasm. He turned to Gabriel. 'Where were you shortly after dinner?'

'I left this room at the same time Shore did. I . . . went from here to an upstairs bathroom.'

'How long were you there?'

'I don't usually clock myself, sir,' the lawyer snapped testily. 'Perhaps twenty minutes. When I left the bathroom, I found the morning paper on the hall table upstairs. I took it into Payne's room and read it. I was waiting for Goode to come back.'

'Goode to come back?'

'I forgot to mention. When I left this room, I went to the kitchen and asked Goode to take my car and run into Warburn. I needed some cigars and some asthma-inhaler. Anything wrong in that?'

'Darby? What happened to you?' Storm asked, ignoring Gabriel's question. The blond man pulled his eyes from Karen. He swallowed and wet his lips.

'I went to the kitchen. Goode hunted

up a bottle of scotch. I went into the living room.'

Storm looked at Walt. 'And you?'

'I stayed in here after the others left. I listened to the symphony for a while, then turned on the news report. I was listening to it when I heard people running down the stairs — '

'By the old Harry!' Gabriel chortled. 'We haven't told Darby about his house — '

'No, we haven't,' Storm snapped. He shifted to face the silent, wax-like figure of the girl. 'Suppose you tell us how you happened to arrive here. And I don't think I know your full name.'

She pulled her eyes from Darby. 'Marini. Karen Marini.' Her voice was low and husky now. 'I called Glenn's house before one o'clock. No one answered. I knew his cousin lived here — that he came over here sometimes. I called here. The man — I think he said he was Goode — he told me Glenn was coming over here this afternoon. I took a train and came out. The taxi brought me from Warburn. I . . . I'd just gotten here.'

She stopped and swallowed. She glanced momentarily at Darby, then at Storm.

'You live in New York, Miss Marini?'

She nodded slightly.

'Was there any particular reason why you visited Mr. Darby today?' Storm wondered absently.

'No, not much,' she said slowly. 'I just wanted to see him . . . ' She paused. Again, her anguished eyes fled to Glenn. 'I knew he needed money. I knew he wouldn't ask me. I came out here to lend him some money,' she explained.

Storm glanced at Darby. Linda saw a flush flow under his cheeks. Storm smiled at Karen. 'That was very kind of you,' he said evenly.

The hall door opened and Goode pushed in a tea cart bearing cups, saucers, coffee, and sandwiches. As the man served, Storm rose and prowled toward the window. He parted the drapes and peered out into the rain-swept darkness. Linda could see the angry frown on his face, the impatient glint in his brown eyes. He turned.

'You went into Warburn to get cigars

for Mr. Gabriel?'

Goode straightened. 'Yes, sir,' he said quickly.

'How long were you away from this house?'

'About thirty minutes in all, sir. I drove quite slowly; not my own car, you see.'

'Did anyone here see anyone leaving this house or returning between two-forty and three-forty?'

There was no answer. Shore ceased stirring his coffee to watch Storm intently. Gabriel blinked owlishly. Walt shook his head. Storm looked at Linda.

'What telephone did you use to call Reddy before dinner?'

'The one outside, in the hall.'

'Was anyone near when you made that call?'

'They were in here,' Linda recalled. 'I heard Uncle Gabe talking about politics and Washington. The door was open.'

'Gabriel and Shore and I were all in here then,' Walt said.

'Did you hear your wife make a telephone call?'

Walt shook his head. 'Gabriel was

talking rather forcefully about that time, I imagine,' he said with a dry smile.

Gabriel leaned forward in his chair, facing Storm. 'Would it be asking entirely too much to inquire what you think you're driving at?' he demanded.

'Not at all,' Storm said acidly. 'I was trying to learn three things: First, who slugged Reddy into unconsciousness and tied him in the basement at two-forty. Second, who then slipped over to Darby's house and set it afire. And, third — '

'Somebody set it afire?' Gabriel echoed.

Storm was looking at Darby. It required at least five seconds for the words to sink into the man's brain. He blinked and blinked again. Then his facial expression seemed to melt into a weak, gray mass. His jaw sagged. 'My . . . house . . . ' he whispered.

'It was burned down this afternoon.'

'It . . . No, you're lying to me!' Darby gripped the chair and heaved himself erect. He swayed and stumbled to the window. He stared into the darkness. He choked and turned. He started across the room to the door. Storm caught him.

'Sit down,' he snapped. 'The burning of

that house may have been the most fortunate thing that ever happened to you.'

'But . . . it's all I've . . . ' He stopped. He stood there, staring at Storm. Then he began to laugh — harshly, loudly. 'Kind of funny . . . funny as hell!' Darby choked as he laughed. 'Kind of like robbing a pauper! Like hitting a — '

'Shut up, Darby!' Storm reached out, and with one hand gripped his shoulder and jerked. Darby's head snapped back. The raw laughter vanished. Slowly, he sagged backward into a chair and mopped his grayish face. The study was filled with a taut, brittle silence as Storm sat down at the desk.

He lit a cigarette deliberately and looked at Reddy. 'You didn't get a look at the person who hit you?'

'No.' The rotund little man's tone was bleak and injured. 'I came down the stairs and started to the door. I'd just passed the first door, the one across the hall into the dining room. I was clipped from behind. I didn't see or hear who it was. The next thing I knew, I was in the basement, tied up. Gagged,' he added bitterly.

Linda watched him pat the back of his head tenderly again.

'Well, I still don't see — ' Gabriel began uncertainly. 'What's the reason for all these goings-on? What's the idea of making such a stir over Darby's shack?'

Storm took a full half-minute to look around the room. When his eyes met Linda's, she felt the almost electric shock of their intensity. And finally he looked squarely at Charles Gabriel.

'Since no one else cares to say, I'll answer that now, Gabriel. Darby's house was destroyed to prevent the identification of Gregory Payne's murderer.'

One moment of charged silence filled the room.

With a wheezing gasp, Gabriel bolted from his chair. 'What did you say? Say that again!' he roared.

'I said that Darby's house was burned to destroy evidence that would have identified Gregory Payne's killer. Payne did *not* commit suicide, Gabriel. He was murdered.'

'But who . . . Why haven't I been informed of this?' the lawyer exploded.

'How do you know? Why haven't . . . The police! Why aren't they here?' he demanded furiously. He stared at Storm. 'This is irregular as all hell!' he roared. 'I demand the police! I intend to call them this instant! I'm doing it now!'

He started across the room. Storm moved not a muscle, save to say coldly:

'Do you think you should, Gabriel?'

Gabriel stopped and spun around. 'What do you mean, sir?'

'I mean this: If you call them, I predict that you'll be under arrest for murder within an hour.'

Gabriel's jaw dropped, and his face turned slowly livid. 'You . . . you jackass! What do you mean by that? Answer me, damn you!'

'I happen to know that you were seen arriving here at a quarter to six on the afternoon Payne was killed — a week ago yesterday, May the thirteenth. Yet when I attempted to question you four days ago, you lied to me. You said you were at your apartment at six o'clock that afternoon.' Storm paused a moment; then as Gabriel remained silent, he continued in the same cold and measured voice:

'And I also know that Payne wrote you a letter, telling you he wished to change his will. I have Payne's carbon copy of that letter. I also have the first copy. Where did I get it?' He cocked a brow gently. 'From a drawer in the bedroom of your apartment, Gabriel. It bears your fingerprints. You had seen, opened, read that letter. And yet this morning on the sunporch you lied to me; you told me you had received no such letter. And Mr. and Mrs. Gordon are here to bear me out.' He paused a long moment, then he gestured toward the hall door.

'I believe you were on your way to call the police.'

Linda's eyes were locked on the fat, heavy-jowled man. His face was turning slowly pasty. The anger was evaporating. A mist of sweat popped across his forehead. Slowly, like a man feeling his way in the dark, he felt his way backward to his chair.

'I . . . can explain,' he breathed. 'I can — '

'Good,' Storm said icily. He looked

about the room. Darby was tense on the edge of his chair, his hands gripping its arms, his bloodshot eyes watching Storm avidly. Walt, too, was taut and alert. Goode, sitting stiffly apart from the others, had ceased mopping his damp face. An expression of vacant anxiety filled his eyes; his mouth was slightly parted. Beside Storm, Karen Marini exhaled a thin breath. And slowly Dr. Shore relaxed, sent a long look of venomous fury at Gabriel, and swallowed. He lit a cigarette.

Storm leaned back in his chair. 'Am I right in assuming that no one here wishes to call the police?' he asked politely.

There was no sound.

Storm leaned forward and nodded to Reddy.

'I believe we are ready now,' he said quietly.

8

James Reddy gave a final pat to the back of his head, then laid the towel aside. He took a dictation pad from his pocket, sat down, and cocked his chair back against the wall. Storm drew a deep breath.

'With the exception of Karen Marini and Mrs. Gordon, everyone in this room has answered certain of my questions before. Unfortunately,' he said drily, 'the answers have been, at times, devoid of truth. Those who have lied are aware of that fact. I hope you will all take this chance to correct the inconsistencies.' He paused and mashed out his cigarette. 'There are three different times and dates that have a positive relationship to this murder-sequence; the first two relate to the attempted murder, and the actual murder, of Gregory Payne. The third bears upon the attempted murder of Linda Gordon.'

There was a soft gasp from someone.

141

'At nine-thirty on the evening of May the twelfth, Friday a week ago, an unsuccessful attempt was made on Payne's life.' He looked squarely at Gabriel. 'Where were you at that hour on the twelfth?'

'I've answered that before. You know I told the truth. I attended a board meeting of the Haliburton Fox Corporation, of which I am a director. That was in New York City.'

Storm nodded almost mechanically. 'And you, Goode?'

'At nine-thirty I was in my rooms above the garage, sir.'

'You heard no disturbance from this house?'

'No, sir. But I frequently play my radio, sir.'

'And, Darby, where were you at nine-thirty that night?'

'I was at home. I was alone. And I can't prove I was there, either,' he said sullenly.

'Shore?' Storm looked intently at the doctor.

'As I've said,' the doctor replied drily, 'I spent the evening with my wife at our apartment. Nor can I prove I was there, beyond my wife's statement.'

'And you, Mr. Gordon, were at the theater in New York with Mrs. Gordon, then Linda Payne.' He leaned forward. 'So, if I'm to believe your stories, only Darby was completely free and near enough to have attempted the murder on May the twelfth. Only Darby and Goode,' he added as an afterthought.

'But I didn't try to kill him, I tell you!' Darby said thickly. 'I told you, I was in my house all evening and night!'

Goode said nothing. He mopped his lined face with his damp handkerchief.

Storm shrugged and lit another cigarette. 'Now we'll move ahead to the late afternoon and early evening of Saturday, May the thirteenth, a week ago yesterday. On that day, between the hours of four in the afternoon and seven in the evening, Gregory Payne was murdered in his bedroom upstairs.' He paused, then looked at Gabriel. 'Are you ready to tell the truth about your visit here that afternoon?'

'Now, see here,' Gabriel said anxiously. 'You're making too much of nothing. The fact is, I . . . came out just before six o'clock on the afternoon of the thirteenth. But I came in response to a telephone call from Payne. The call reached me at my office, just as I was going to lunch at one o'clock. He said he wanted to discuss a few changes in his will. He asked me to drive out that afternoon. I did. But,' he added firmly and heavily, 'I did *not* enter this house that afternoon.'

'Why not?' Storm inquired.

'The house was locked, back and front. I knocked and called. I got no answer. After ten minutes of that, I decided I must have misunderstood the call. I returned to New York.'

'And why didn't you mention your visit when I questioned you four days ago?'

'Well, I . . . No need to rock the boat, I decided. You see, I learned the next day that Payne had committed suicide. I . . . You can see my point,' he exploded uneasily. 'I'm the executor of the man's estate. He's dead. He's mentioned changes, but I haven't the slightest idea what changes he had in mind. What can I do?' He spread his massive hands emptily. 'Nothing. Nothing at all! The best thing to do is leave everything at peace, I said. Nobody is disturbed that way. No doubts or uncertainties. Just a normal will to be executed.' He mopped his damp jowls and looked appealingly at Storm. 'You would have done the same thing in my position, yes?' Again he mopped his jowls. 'After all, I had no hint that Payne's death was murder.'

'And so, to avoid any disturbance,' Storm supplied ironically, 'you took Payne's letter from your files and carried it to your home — doubtless intending to destroy it.'

'Well, er . . . Yes. You . . . you put it in the worst light.'

'Candidly, Gabriel,' Storm said, 'didn't you also consider the chance that Payne might have planned to rule you out of his will, thus losing you twenty-five thousand dollars?'

'See here, sir!' the man roared. 'I'm not a . . . a criminal! I have means! I gave no thought to such a possibility!'

'Very well,' Storm accepted with a dry smile. 'And what time did you say Payne called you to come out here?'

'It was about noon — just a little after noon. I worked that afternoon in my office, alone.'

Storm glanced at Reddy. The man nodded.

'Where were you, Darby, between four and seven o'clock on the thirteenth?' Storm asked.

'I was . . . was . . . ' he started slowly.

'That was Saturday before last?' Karen asked quickly. 'He was with me in New York. We met at five o'clock at Grand Central Station, and went to dinner. After that, we went to a show, then to my hotel. He was with me all the time until midnight. All the time,' she repeated earnestly.

Storm tapped the desk. 'Where in New York do you live?'

'I . . . ' She paused. For one instant her eyes met Glenn's. 'At the Golden Owl Hotel on Third Avenue,' she said softly.

'Yet you, Glenn, told me you spent that evening alone in New York,' Storm reminded the blond man.

'I was just trying to keep Karen out of

anything,' Darby snapped. 'But you'll find people who'll swear I was in New York.'

'I have. But where were you early in the afternoon? For instance, it takes thirty minutes from Warburn to Grand Central by train. You arrived at five. That leaves the time between four and four-thirty in which you could have killed Payne.'

'But I was at home dressing at that time, and then getting to the station. And at two in the afternoon I was in Warburn getting a haircut. You can prove that. I was in town over an hour, in fact.'

'You know,' Gabriel said suddenly, 'that name, that Golden Owl . . . I've heard that name somewhere before. Seems as if I had a case involving that place, but . . . But it's strange I'd have had anything concerning a Third Avenue hotel,' he added fretfully.

Storm quirked his brows. Linda heard Glenn's chair creak as he leaned forward sharply. A half-gasp slipped from his lips. Storm glanced around, then peered quickly at Karen. The girl, like Glenn, was tense in her chair. She was watching Gabriel with taut anxiety.

Linda saw Storm's lips move.

'What is the — ' He stopped abruptly.

He pulled a scrap of paper and pencil from his pocket and scrawled a few words. He motioned to Reddy. The man approached the desk and peered at the scrap of paper. He glanced at Storm, nodded, took the paper. He started toward the hall door.

'Use the upstairs phone,' Storm said. James Reddy nodded and left the room, closing the door behind him. Storm turned toward Shore. 'Where were you between those certain hours of the thirteenth?'

'As I've told you, I left Constancy Hospital at four-thirty. I arrived at my apartment around five. My wife was there. We were alone; incidentally, we haven't had a servant since last fall. I spent the rest of the thirteenth at home with my wife.'

Storm nodded and looked at Walt. 'Where were you?'

Linda saw her husband frown slightly. 'Well, I telephoned you at about five that afternoon, and we met at the Alastaire

Club for a drink; then we went to dinner. We didn't get through until almost eight. And between four and five, I . . . Just at my apartment,' he said finally. 'I spent some time composing. I showered and dressed just before I called you. That's about the best I can do.'

Storm nodded and looked at Goode questioningly. The man pulled himself erect and swallowed nervously. 'I had been given a vacation, you know, sir. Mr. Payne intended going into New York. I had gone to Warburn the morning of the thirteenth and purchased his ticket for the seven-ten train that evening. At the same time, I'd gotten a ticket for myself on the three-thirty train to Albany.' He smiled restlessly and gestured. 'I came back to the house. I prepared lunch for Mr. Payne. At two you arrived, sir. At about three, you left. Shortly thereafter I left in a taxi for Warburn — at three-ten, I would say. I was on the three-thirty train that left Warburn for Albany.'

'I see. So,' Storm mused, 'if I am to believe your stories, there are three people in this room who could have murdered

149

Gregory Payne. You, Gabriel, could have done it when you came to this house that evening at six o'clock. You, Mr. Gordon, could have done it and gotten back to New York in time to make the call to me at five. And you, Darby, could have done it before you took the train for New York and met Karen Marini.'

He paused a moment. 'Now, when we put the two dates together, the nine-thirty time on the twelfth and the murder period of the thirteenth, we find that only one person in this room was free to murder and to attempt to murder on those dates . . . if I am to believe your stories. That one person is Glenn Darby.'

'But I didn't do it! I tell you, I didn't kill — ' Darby started wildly.

'Sit down. Be still,' Storm snapped. 'I'm not through.' He loosened his collar slightly and took a deep breath. 'Now, I'm interested in the last of the three times and dates. To be exact, ten o'clock last night.' He looked at Walt. 'I know where you were. And you,' he added to Gabriel. He nodded toward Darby. 'I know where you say you were,' he went on with a touch of irony. 'And you were in the kitchen, Goode?'

The man nodded quickly. He continued to mop his face uneasily.

'And where were you at ten last night, Dr. Shore?' Storm asked.

'Ten? Last night?' Shore echoed the words strangely. Slowly, he straightened from his slumped position in his chair. 'I . . . At ten,' he repeated hollowly. 'I was in Warburn at ten,' he said.

Storm's brows went up. 'Doing what?'

'I . . . I got a call. The call came to me at my apartment around nine last night. It was from the Warburn exchange. The speaker was a man — he said his name was Hilton. He said he'd been a close friend of Linda's. His wife was ill, quite ill, he said. He knew no doctors, but he remembered hearing Linda mention me. He asked . . . implored me to come out and examine his wife. He gave me an address. I . . . Purely on the basis of his friendship with Linda, I made the trip.' Shore paused to swallow heavily.

'But I don't know anyone named Hilton!' Linda exclaimed.

'I . . . I couldn't find the address he'd given me. There was no such street in Warburn,' Shore explained jerkily. 'I stopped at a garage and asked. There was no Hilton in the phone book, either. At last, I gave up and returned to New York. I got home after eleven.'

'From nine until eleven,' Storm mused aloud. 'And did you pass this house during that time?'

'No,' Shore said flatly. 'I was never within half a mile of this house. Nor did I know that Linda had returned — I learned that when I got home.' The doctor fumbled for his handkerchief. He was watching Storm anxiously. 'You . . . when you started this questioning, you said that the third date related to the attempted murder of Linda. Do you mean that . . . last night at ten . . . ' he whispered.

'I do,' Storm said quietly. 'At ten last night a shot was fired; a shot that, save for a freak of luck, would have killed Mrs. Gordon.'

'Oh.' Shore's lips twitched. He glanced at Linda, then back at Storm. 'But that call . . . I swear to God I got it.'

'Very well,' Storm accepted drily. 'Then, putting the three dates together, and believing everything that each person has said here tonight, we find that there is no person in this room who was free to take part in the three actions — in all of them. So at least one person is lying,' he said slowly. 'I know who that person is. He — '

The door opened and James Reddy entered. His eyes were bright and his cheeks flushed. 'It was a good hunch,' he said. 'A guy with that name lives there.'

Storm's brows arched. 'Was he there?'

Reddy shook his head. 'But I called Fitzhugh at Police Identification and got a load about him. Very interesting.'

Storm glanced at the clock on the mantel. It was ten-fifteen. He rose abruptly. 'I'll have to ask everyone to remain in this house tonight. I'll contact your apartments and explain. I'll also have to ask you to double up. Gabriel, you will room with Darby. Mr. Gordon, I'll ask you to stay with Dr. Shore. Goode, you may stay in your quarters alone, and Miss Marini will take the room adjoining Mrs. Gordon's, please. Will you show the gentlemen to their rooms, Goode?'

'Now, see here, Storm,' Gabriel began peevishly. 'Is all this to-do necessary? I fail to see — '

'It is quite necessary, I assure you. If you will accompany Goode . . . '

The lawyer flushed and heaved himself to his feet. Shore and Darby rose. The blond man sent a restless glance at Karen, then looked at Storm. Walt rose and smiled wearily at Linda.

'Be careful, darling,' he said quietly. He clasped her fingers a moment, then straightened and followed the others from the room. Linda heard their footsteps moving in the upper hall, heard doors opening and closing. Presently, Goode returned.

'That will be all,' Storm said. 'Close the door as you leave.'

'Yes, sir.' The man departed, leaving Linda with Karen, Reddy, and Storm. The detective turned his chair to face Karen.

'You love Glenn Darby, don't you, Karen?' he asked quietly.

The girl looked at him steadily. 'Is there

anything wrong in that?'

'Please. I'm trying to help you. I know you didn't come here this afternoon to lend Darby money. You came here to give him some message involving what happened last night.' He paused. 'Didn't you?' he prompted patiently.

'No! I tell you, no!'

Storm's hand moved forward. Swiftly and deftly, he extracted a small beaded handbag from her pocket. The girl gasped, and clutched at his arm. Storm shook his head. Deliberately, he opened the bag and emptied the contents onto the desk.

There was a handkerchief, a single key, a compact, two lipsticks, a comb, and eight dollars. Storm looked back to the girl. 'You came all the way from New York in a storm to lend Darby eight dollars?' he asked softly.

'But I . . . I was just going to tell him — tell him I would lend him some money if he needed it.'

'Why couldn't you have phoned him?'

The girl swallowed and twisted her fingers together.

Storm leaned forward. 'Stop trying to

deceive me, Miss Marini. I'll be honest with you. I overhead you trying to rouse Darby in the living room. You were trying to tell him something about what happened last night. Your message involved a man whose name is Coke. He — '

'Oh!' The girl's fingers flew to her throat. Her eyes widened. 'You heard . . . know about — '

'I heard,' Storm agreed patiently. 'And a while ago you and Darby both showed anxiety when the Golden Owl Hotel was mentioned. I asked Reddy to call the hotel. He did. I know that a Mr. Coke Brill lives there.' He turned to Reddy. 'What did Fitzhugh tell you about Brill?'

'The guy runs a night club called the Sparrow Inn on East Thirty-Third. He did a short hitch for bootlegging in Prohibition. Since then, they haven't tagged him for keeps, but Fitzhugh did some hinting that Brill is in the narcotics racket now.'

Storm arched a brow. 'And didn't Darby have trouble with dope? Didn't Gabriel defend him? And wasn't Gabriel trying to remember where he'd heard the name Golden Owl?' He waited a pointed

156

moment as he watched Karen's tense face. 'What goes on between Darby and Brill, Karen?' he asked flatly.

The girl shook her head furiously. 'I don't know! Glenn doesn't even know Brill!'

'Quit lying to me!' Storm exploded angrily. 'The story of Darby's fight Saturday night is an absurdity. The fact that he carefully kept the ring with the hair and blood indicates that he *knew* he'd be needing evidence to prove that an absurdity was a reality. And you know — '

'No, no! I tell you, I don't!' the girl almost screamed. 'Leave me alone! I don't . . . we don't know anything! Glenn didn't do it — didn't kill anybody! Isn't that enough?' she choked.

'It's a long way from enough,' Storm snapped. 'But perhaps Brill will tell the truth.'

'You . . . You're not going after him?' Karen breathed starkly.

'Why shouldn't I?'

'But you . . . He'll tell . . . No!' she gasped, half-rising from her chair. Her eyes were aflame with fright. Her lips worked as though she were being strangled. 'You can't! He'll lie . . . and about the woman . . . the body . . . He'll tell you that Glenn — ' She stopped. An expression of stricken horror spread across her face.

'But I know all about the woman's body,' Storm said quietly. 'I watched Glenn go to the grave. Now . . . won't you tell me what happened Saturday — '

'Oh!' Linda cried sharply. She started forward.

Reddy caught the girl as she collapsed. Storm exhaled a long breath and rose.

'She'll be all right,' he said wearily. 'Take her up to Mrs. Gordon's room. Stay there until Mrs. Gordon comes.'

Linda watched Reddy depart with the slender, limp figure in his arms, then she looked at Storm. 'That wasn't very kind of you,' she said, almost angrily. 'You could see how she was.'

'I know.' Storm shrugged listlessly. 'But there wasn't much kindness in the murder of your father. Or of that poor Walker woman, either,' he said. He looked at her soberly. 'You lose the gentle touch when you take a beating. I should have stayed with that corpse. I shouldn't have taken the slightest chance. But damn it, who would have expected anybody to steal it?' he demanded in bitter self-reproach.

Linda blinked. 'I . . . What do you mean?' she asked strangely.

'The corpse in the well. I . . . Oh, I hadn't told you,' he remembered. 'It was stolen from the hole while we were upstairs talking in the afternoon. It was moved to Darby's house and the house was burned to destroy the corpse.'

'That thing . . . It was *moved*! Burned!' Linda gasped.

Storm nodded. 'And why I — ' he stopped as the telephone in the hall rang. Swiftly he left the room. Linda heard him speaking. 'Yes . . . Hello, Elsie . . . You did!' His voice sharpened with excitement. 'Good! Bring it out here. You know the address . . . ? Fine, good work, Elsie!' The receiver clicked down. Storm returned.

'At least one thing goes right,' he announced. 'My secretary located a mustard-yellow suitcase at Pennsylvania Station. It had been removed from an automatic locker box when the time limit expired. The description of the contents I gave her fitted almost perfectly. There were two plain dresses scented with lilac, a pair of sturdy shoes, size seven, some toilet articles, and three pairs of step-ins. But the bag contains no slips or brassieres!'

'The woman's bag!' Linda exclaimed.

'And the same enigma: Why are there no slips or brassieres?'

Linda frowned. 'I don't understand. A woman that age, it seems . . . ' she mused aloud.

'Well, that's all for now. You may as well go to bed. I've had Karen put in the room adjoining yours; she'll use your bath, but I don't think you need to worry about her. Lock the door if you're afraid.'

'Oh, I'm not. There's something pathetic about her.' Linda moved toward the door. As she touched the knob, she hesitated and turned back. 'You know, you said someone was lying. You said you knew who the man was.'

Storm nodded. 'Please don't ask me to tell you who.'

'I just . . . It isn't Walt?' she broke out anxiously.

He smiled reassuringly. 'No. I can promise you it wasn't Walt.'

Linda breathed deeply. 'That's all I wanted to know. I'm afraid my whole perspective . . . everything's getting tangled up. I'll be glad when this is over,' she said sincerely. She opened the door. 'Good night, Mr. Storm.'

'Good night, Mrs. Gordon.'

She closed the door and turned toward the stairs.

9

James Reddy glanced at Linda from the bathroom as she entered her bedroom. He breathed a sigh of relief. 'Look, you'll do better at this. You call me in case you need me.' He jerked a thumb toward the still, thin figure of Karen on the bed in the adjoining room, then laid aside a damp towel and scurried from the room.

Linda wet the towel with cold water and laid it across the girl's forehead. Karen did not move. Linda returned to her own bedroom, locked the hall door. As she began to undress slowly, she realized how completely tired she was. Her head ached dully. Her mind was confused as she tried to recall the events of the day. One fragment of vivid recollection remained — the arm, soiled and thin and white.

She closed her eyes a moment. She sat down at the dresser and began to brush her hair.

The bed in the next room creaked. She turned. Karen was leaning through the doorway, her lips pale and parted, her eyes startled. She stared around Linda's room, and her eyes settled on the other woman. They puzzled an instant, then a cloud of recollection filled their depths.

'You feel better now?' Linda asked quickly. 'I'll help you — '

'Storm? Where is he?' Karen whispered.

'He's downstairs.'

'Oh.' The girl swallowed.

Linda opened a drawer and took out a pair of pajamas. 'If you'd like, I'll help you put on — '

'Oh, no,' Karen said swiftly. 'I don't . . . can't sleep.'

'You'll have to try, please,' Linda argued gently.

'I'm all right now.' She pushed Linda away and continued to stare about the room, her restless eyes hunting, searching, while their dark depths struggled with uncertain thoughts. 'What time is it?' she asked.

'After ten.' Linda looked at her

uneasily. 'You've got to go to bed,' she said finally. 'I am. You might as well, anyway. Storm won't let you leave here tonight, you know.'

'No. No, I . . . guess he won't,' she whispered. 'I . . . Yes, I'll go to bed.' She hesitated, then picked up the pajamas, and entered the bathroom, closing the door behind her. Linda frowned at the closed door, and some curious echo of the girl's words lingered in her ears.

At last she finished undressing, put on her pajamas, and turned out the light. She felt her way to bed.

The room was still. Linda stared upward at the dark ceiling. She heard the monotonously regular dripping of the rain through the gutters of the house. She heard the tree limbs scratch listlessly against the cornice. From downstairs she heard a door closing firmly. Then she listened to the silence and the endless drip-drip of the rain. And as she lay there, her mind roamed to the rooms along the hall — to the people who slept beneath this same roof. And she wondered . . .

She remembered that she hadn't locked

the door to the bathroom. Was there any use? She felt no fear of Karen; only pity.

She didn't know how long it was before she heard the slight, soft, clicking sound from the bathroom. Next, she felt an almost imperceptible movement of air in the dark room; she knew the bathroom door had been opened. Next, she heard the soft whisper of bare feet across the floor. She lay still, scarcely breathing as she waited and listened in the darkness.

The footsteps were searching their way in the direction of the dresser. They stopped. Then came a muffled metallic sound, as though a few coins had been rattled together. Finally she heard the cautious turning of the key in the lock of the hall door. The air moved again in the room. The hinges whined. She heard the door close. Karen had left the room, she knew.

Carefully, Linda pushed back the covers and rose, feeling her way across the room to the hall door. She listened. She heard Karen's voice murmuring guardedly:

'Stillwater 4-4996, please . . . ' There

was a long silence. 'Mr. Brill, please . . . Coke . . . ? It's Karen. I can't talk much. You'll have to listen . . . No, I'm at the Payne house . . . Yes . . . Listen, Coke; the detective knows it all. All about you and the body in the hole . . . Yes, I swear to God he knows . . . I've got to talk to you, see you as quick as I can . . . No, he knows about the Golden Owl, too . . . No, how about the apartment uptown? Is anyone there . . . ? Then I'll meet you there in less than an hour. Goodbye.'

There was silence. Linda still heard the rain in the gutters. Then she heard the soft footsteps moving . . . moving along the hall in the direction of the stairs. She heard them descending slowly.

Swiftly she stumbled across the room, pulling off her pajamas as she went. She fumbled into the closet and plunged her arms into a sweater. She found part of her underwear, a skirt, and her shoes. Rapidly, she pulled the clothes on. She did not put on the shoes. She carried them in her hands as she silently opened the door and tiptoed into the hall.

Down the steps she felt her way, into the lower hall. Still there was no sound, no light save the crack that shone beneath the closed study door. Quickly, she turned the knob.

'Storm! Quick, Karen's going to — '

She stopped. The room was empty. Nothing moved but the veil of cigarette smoke that drifted about the ceiling. She turned back down the hall.

'Storm! Storm!' she called anxiously. She hurried into the kitchen. 'Storm!' she shouted.

The door of a car slammed solidly. A moment later a motor coughed and roared. Tires spun and gravel rattled in the driveway. And Linda watched her own coupé flash through the darkness and go racing into the night.

'Storm! Storm, where are — ' she shouted wildly.

'Here! What is it?' Storm's voice shouted distantly.

She heard steps thundering across the wooden bridge at the creek. She ran from the sunporch across the driveway. She met him halfway to the garage.

'It's Karen! She got away in my car! Going to that man named Brill! I heard her phoning him and — '

'Tell me later! Come on!' He grabbed her hand, almost lifting her off her feet as he plunged toward his own car. Linda leaped in and slammed the door. An instant later the motor was roaring. The car cut a curve across the lawn, smashed through a hedge, and tore down the drive. Storm left the lights off and hunched over the wheel. The slightest mist of moonlight was filtering through the thinning clouds. The high front hedge flashed past Linda's eyes, and the car swayed drunkenly into the highway. Far ahead down the ribbon of concrete, Linda saw two tiny red dots — the taillights of the coupé.

'Where was Reddy?' Storm demanded harshly. 'I put him in that upstairs hall. He should have tagged her.'

'I didn't see or hear him at all. The lights were off. I . . . I heard Karen coming into my room from the bath. I'd forgotten to lock the door. I heard her stop at the dresser and rattle . . . Oh, she was getting the keys to the coupé! I remember they were there; she must have noticed them. Then she slipped into the hall and called a New York number. She talked to that man Brill. She said you knew about everything — him and the body in the well. She said she'd meet him at a place called the uptown apartment in less than an hour. Then she slipped down the stairs. I followed.'

Storm grunted. 'My cigarettes. In the pocket there. Get down low and light one for me.' He still had not turned on the lights, and he was keeping the same distance between his car and Linda's. 'You saw nothing of Reddy all that time?' he asked again.

'Nothing.' Linda handed him the lighted cigarette.

'Something happened to him,' Storm said anxiously. 'He was in that hall, beside that phone, thirty minutes ago when I went over to the ruins of Darby's house.'

'You were over there?' Linda echoed.

Storm grunted. 'There and at the grave,' he said tersely. He was leaning forward again. Linda glanced at the speedometer. The indicator hovered around sixty. She glanced up as the dark shopping section of Warburn slid out of the night, then faded past. The speedometer climbed slowly. The deep song of the motor filled Linda's ears. Her eyes were fixed on the tiny dots of red dancing in the darkness far ahead.

It seemed to Linda that scarcely a minute had passed before they were roaring through Yonkers, past the ever-thickening houses. The car sped into upper Broadway, and a rattling streetcar reminded Linda that they were in New York City

The speedometer needle began to drop back. The red taillights became more distinct as the space between the two cars narrowed. On and on, deeper into New York, Karen drove. She turned into the West Side highway.

'I thought you said something about an uptown apartment,' Storm grunted softly.

'I did. That's what I heard her say.'

Storm shook his head. 'Looks like we're headed for something farther down.'

Linda held her breath as the coupé wove out of sight, breathing again as she found the taillights.

'There she goes,' Storm murmured as the coupé swung down into a cross street. He turned in behind her. He was scarcely fifty feet behind her when they crossed Times Square and continued over toward the East Side. At Third Avenue, Karen turned downtown again.

'Looks like she's headed for the Golden Owl,' he said.

'But she told him they couldn't go there,' Linda countered.

'Maybe she's got another reason all her own. We'll see. If . . . Yes. Look. Stopping,' he said gently. 'And there's the Golden Owl.'

Linda glanced across the street. On the corner was a massive five-story building; old and ill-kept. Storm slipped the car into the curb. Across the dark street, and under the giant skeleton of the Elevated, Karen hurried. She vanished into the entrance of the Golden Owl. Storm opened his door and stepped out.

'Wait here,' he said. He cut across the street and was lost in the deeper darkness of the side-street. Linda's eyes returned to the entrance of the hotel. It was lit by a pale bluish light and she could see a section of stairs rising just within the doors. Farther down the street was the only lighted shop — a bar. A dim red neon sign winked dirtily, outlining a beer bottle, and the faint music of a tango drifted through the night. Two men came out of the bar and their heavy voices argued off into the distance. The men disappeared. The tango ended. Linda felt the brutal silence beneath the hulking spans of the El. She shivered, staring back toward the Golden Owl.

From the bar came the music of a Hawaiian record. Fragments of the words drifted to Linda's ears. It was an old love song. And for a fragile moment she slipped back to a day that was not yet a week old. She was standing with Walt in a tiny stucco house in New Mexico. Before them stood a little man with a bible. Linda could see his lips moving; she could hear his words exactly: 'And do you, Linda Payne, take this man to be your lawful wedded husband, in sickness . . . '

The music ended. Linda found herself still staring at the pale-blue entrance of the Golden Owl. Then, softly, she sobbed. 'Oh, God,' she whispered. She didn't know just why she had said it, or exactly what she had meant.

She had no time to think of it again. Karen Marini came hurrying from the hotel, crossed the street, slipped inside the coupé. The motor roared throatily. Abruptly, the shadow of Storm appeared and slid into the car beside Linda. A moment later the motor was singing. The car was moving after Karen.

The coupé turned into a side street and headed across Manhattan. At Fifth Avenue it turned uptown. They followed. Karen drove past Central Park until, at 110th Street, she turned west again. Past the fringe of Harlem they drove, across Broadway. And, between Riverside Drive and Broadway, Karen pulled the coupé into the darkness near tall apartment buildings. Storm stopped a hundred feet behind her.

Linda saw the slender girl glancing up toward the windows of some upper apartment. Then she hurried through a doorway.

Storm opened his door and got out. He

hesitated. 'You'd better come along. If we hear anything, two statements are better than one. Hurry.'

Linda slipped out. She followed Storm to the edge of the doorway. He stopped and peered around the corner. He moved on and Linda followed. They crossed an over-decorated lobby of marble and chrome. The one night elevator was up. Linda heard the cables clanking in the shaft. She heard a door rattle open somewhere above. It closed. Presently, the lights of the elevator appeared beyond the closed doors. The door opened. Storm and Linda entered.

'Which floor did she go to?' Storm asked quietly. The boy at the control turned. His eyes travelled down Storm's arm. They widened. And Linda saw that Storm was holding a ten-dollar bill in his fingers. The boy smiled.

'Number six, sir.' His fingers closed on the bill.

'What apartment?'

The boy hesitated, frowning.

'I won't remember where I found out,' Storm said.

'It's the one at the front, sir. Number Six-A.'

'We'll get off at the fifth. And what about the door? Is it locked?' As Storm asked the question, he drew another bill from his pocket. The boy's eyes fixed on it for a moment. 'Maybe you have a key that will fit?' Storm suggested softly.

'I'll tell you, sir,' the boy said cautiously, 'just between me and you, I know about that set-up in Six-A.' A sly grin crossed his lips. 'I think I can maybe fix you with a key if you — '

'If I can forget. And I can,' Storm said easily. The boy reached into his pocket, selected a key and removed it from the ring, and the bill left Storm's fingers. He took the key. The elevator rose to the fifth floor.

Linda followed him down the hall to the stairway. He stopped on the landing between the floors. From inside his coat he took a gun, examined it, and then returned it to his pocket.

'Stay behind me. Don't make any noise,' he whispered. They climbed the last steps and moved along the sixth floor

175

hall to the front door, Six-A. The key grated slightly in the lock. Linda realized that her lungs were starved for air. She breathed thinly.

'She got a gun at the Golden Owl,' Storm whispered. 'I . . . '

Linda's muscles tightened as she heard the lock click softly. Storm glanced at her and his lips formed a silent word: *Slow*.

Inch by cautious inch, he opened the door until Linda could look into a portion of hallway. From the depths of the hall came light. Storm drew the gun from his pocket. His left hand sealed itself on Linda's arm. Slowly, he entered the hall, drawing her behind him. Gently, he closed the door, and Linda heard him suck in a breath. And yet there was no sound in the apartment.

He began to move along the wall. Six feet ahead, on the left, was a wide archway into an unlit room. Storm left the hall and entered the room. Linda followed. By the light from the hall, she saw that the room was the living room. There was a radio. In the shadows she saw a table, chairs.

Storm continued to move toward another door that opened off the living room. No light shone beneath the door. Linda heard the latch click. She felt rather than saw the door open into darkness. And then, for the first time, she heard a soft footstep in some deeper room of the apartment. She thought she heard a drawer closing. There was no other sound.

Linda waited for Storm to move again. He made no motion. It seemed to her that they waited an eternity. She felt Storm's fingers bite hard into the flesh of her arm.

And the gentle clicking of the hall door came again — came as the door was cautiously opened. The slightest scuff of footsteps moved along the hall floor as someone went tiptoeing toward the rear of the apartment. A silent moment passed, then a door opened.

'Yeah?' a man's deep, organ-like voice said quickly. 'I'm late. What busted out there? How did you — ?'

'Don't come any closer, Coke,' Karen's brittle quiet voice spoke. 'Don't! I mean it!'

'Huh? What is it?' the man asked

177

suspiciously. 'What's the rod for?'

'To kill you.'

A long moment passed. 'Oh,' he murmured. 'Like that?'

'Just like that, Coke,' she said deliberately. Storm moved. Linda followed as he felt his way across the dark room to another door. Linda heard the man speaking as Storm opened the door. She peered into the darkness of this room, and saw the margin of light shining under another door. Now the voices were near, muted yet distinct. The man was speaking:

' . . . and you think you can get away with it?'

'I'm not even going to try.'

'Don't be a fool! What reason have you got to — ?'

'You wouldn't understand the reasons. You never understand — '

'What's in you? Don't tell me you're playing for the yellow-haired chump!'

'I'm not telling anything. I'm just going to kill you. I'll pick up that phone and call the cops. I'll tell 'em what you were, and how and where I fitted. It won't make any difference who believes me or if they don't. You won't be around to tell about that woman.'

'So it *is* the yellow-haired boy! What in hell do you see — '

Storm touched the knob of the door behind which Karen was speaking. Linda stood still, stiff, breathless. Abruptly, the latch clicked. The door swung inward, spreading a ribbon of light across the dark floor. Linda caught a glimpse of Storm and his gun as he stepped through the doorway. She heard a startled gasp from Karen, a choked curse from the man. Storm was speaking:

'Drop it, Karen! Don't move, Brill! Don't move!'

'You! Oh, God . . . how did . . . ' Karen breathed.

Linda heard a heavy object bump to the floor. Slowly, she edged to the open door. She saw Karen standing rigid in the middle of the room. At her feet lay a small, flat automatic. Storm stood beside her, his left hand locked on the girl's thin wrist. His gun pointed across the room. Linda's eyes followed its direction. She saw Brill — a large man, almost as fat as Gabriel.

'So it was just a little trap, wasn't it, Karen?' he was murmuring ironically. His lips were thick and sensual. His eyes were round and pale-blue. He was expensively dressed in a gray-striped suit, and a fringe of gray hair showed beneath the brim of his pearl-gray hat. His face was austere but flabby. He was about fifty, Linda guessed, with small, white hands and a paunch.

'Lift your arms, Brill. Turn around. Slowly,' Storm ordered.

Brill's mouth twitched drily. He wet his lips with his tongue. 'Sure,' he said deliberately. 'Anything you say.' As he turned, his pale eyes raked over Karen with deadly fury. His hands went up above his shoulders. Storm stooped, pocketed the gun on the floor, and cautiously approached Brill from behind.

His hand moved into Brill's pockets. Linda saw him remove a gun, a billfold, and keys. Storm crammed them into his own pockets and retreated to the middle of the room.

'Did he kill Gregory Payne, Karen?' he asked quietly.

The girl's pale lips trembled. No word came.

'You can tell me the truth,' Storm promised. 'I know Glenn didn't kill the woman.'

Karen's eyes opened wide with startled surprise. 'You . . . *know*?'

'I think so.' He looked at her steadily. 'Did Brill kill Gregory Payne?'

Almost imperceptibly the girl nodded. 'Yes. Yes,' she whispered.

Brill jerked and half turned. 'That's a lie! You're not going to believe that dope-headed little — '

'I think I am, Brill,' Storm said drily. 'Linda,' he went on, 'you and Karen go first. Use the stairs. We'll take my car. You drive, Linda. Sit in front with her, Karen.'

'Where are we going?' Brill asked shortly.

'To Mrs. Gordon's. Start walking, Brill. Keep your hands up and move slowly.'

Brill's fury-filled pale eyes fixed themselves on Karen for one long moment. 'So you traded me for the golden-haired punk,' he breathed. His lips formed one more silent word, then he turned stiffly and moved.

10

It was ten minutes to two in the morning when Linda followed Storm, Brill, and Karen across the driveway toward the door of the sunporch. The lights shone from the kitchen, from the dining room. The light was on in the upper hall.

They entered the downstairs hall, and the study door opened. James Reddy's bald head appeared. 'Who is — ' The question died away as he stared at Brill; then, glancing at Storm and nodding toward Brill, he asked: 'Where did you get *that*?'

'Where were you when you were supposed to be in the upstairs hall?' Storm countered testily.

'Taking a walk along the creek. One of the guests got restless.' He gestured into the study. Storm moved Brill through the doorway. Karen followed them stiffly. As Linda entered she saw the figure of Dr. Clifton Shore hunched in a chair. He was

183

clad in an undershirt, house shoes, and trousers. His eyes lifted to Storm. Linda almost gasped.

The doctor's face was a ghastly white. The dark eyes were sick and vacant. His entire expression was one of utter dejection.

'Well,' Storm murmured, looking at Reddy, 'so Dr. Shore went for a walk?'

'He dropped by his car and lifted a gun from the dashboard compartment, then strolled down the creek and tossed it in.'

Storm cocked a brow. 'Very interesting. That makes two interesting explanations that we are about to hear. Sit down, Brill.' His eyes paused a moment on a cheap imitation-leather suitcase that stood against the wall. 'Elsie here?' he asked Reddy.

The man nodded. 'Upstairs in the hall, just in case.'

'Go up and bring everyone down,' he ordered. He gestured Karen into a chair. Linda sat down near the desk, and Storm sat down behind it. He laid his gun on the edge of the desk and looked at Shore wearily. 'You should have told me the truth about that gun,' he remarked absently. 'I searched your car early yesterday evening. I knew it was there. And I found the binder of Payne's missing Encyclopedia volume in your closet at your apartment three days ago.' He gestured slightly. 'I mention these things in the hope of overcoming your reluctance to talk. Not,' he added, 'that it will make a great deal of difference anymore.'

Shore swallowed. His face in the harsh light from above was gaunt and seemingly lifeless. He sagged back in his chair and closed his eyes hopelessly. From the stairs came the sound of muttering voices, descending feet. The door opened.

Walt entered first, clad in a robe. His face was sleep-stained, his hair rumpled. He stared about the room and his eyes widened as he saw that Linda was dressed and wide awake. Behind him came Gabriel, bundled in pajamas and the trousers of his suit. His face seemed strangely naked without his glasses. After the lawyer came Glenn Darby. He started through the doorway, saw Brill, and stopped as though he had smashed into a wall. His eyes flared wide and a strangled gasp escaped his lips.

'Sit down, Darby. All of you, sit down,' Storm ordered.

Goode edged into the room, hurriedly buttoning a collarless shirt, then sat down gingerly on the edge of a stiff chair. The door began to close before Reddy came in with a small, plain-faced girl of about twenty-five. Her hair was reddish-brown, her eyes clear and bold. Her face and her manner were quiet and competent. She nodded to Storm.

'Get ready to take this down, Elsie,' he said. 'Reddy has a pad and pencil.' He waited a moment, then motioned Reddy into a position that faced the silent semicircle of waiting people. He lit a cigarette, glanced first at Shore, then at Brill, then back to Shore.

'That gun you disposed of,' he began deliberately, 'had recently been fired. One bullet was missing. I noted that when I searched your car in the evening. Furthermore, the binder of the Encyclopedia that I found in your closet was of volume Number Twenty-Two, from 'Text to Vase.' That same volume is missing from Gregory Payne's bookcase in his bedroom. And,' he added pointedly, 'I visited Payne in that bedroom between two and three of the afternoon he was murdered. That volume was in his bookcase then. I demand to know how it got in your bedroom closet, and I want to know why all the pages have been torn out.' He paused and hunched forward. 'I want to know why you disposed of that gun, and how the missing bullet was used.'

'I . . . I don't know how it was used,' Shore said heavily. 'That's why I had . . . had to get rid of it. I didn't know, but I was afraid. I knew I hadn't shot it, but it was gone. I thought of that fake call that brought me to Warburn last Saturday night. And I . . . was afraid,' he said emptily.

'You were afraid your gun had fired the shot at Linda Gordon?' Storm asked.

Shore nodded and pulled himself to the edge of his chair to gesture anxiously. 'You see, Storm,' he breathed harshly, 'I am a victim! I was framed for Gregory

Payne's murder! I was here late that afternoon! I was framed, and I tried to destroy the evidence!'

'Tell me the whole story, Shore,' Storm directed.

'It was five o'clock in the afternoon of the thirteenth. I was at home in my New York apartment.' He paused to mop his sweat-stained face with the back of his hand, then his words came tumbling out in a frantic breathless wave. 'I got a telephone call. The caller, a man, said he was Gregory Payne. It didn't sound like Payne, and I said so. He said he was ill — he said a severe pain; he said he wanted me to look him over at once. He asked me to come out immediately. I . . . Naturally, I did. I arrived at this house a little after six. I found the house locked. I got no answer either here or at Goode's quarters. I suppose I'd have given up, but I recalled that Payne had said he was quite ill. I feared he might have collapsed. I . . . I used my keys. I was able to open the sunporch door into the kitchen. I went through the lower part of the house, found nothing; went upstairs. I found Payne in his bedroom, stretched across his bed. There was a wound in his right temple. He was dead — had been dead for well over an hour, I could see. Perhaps an hour and a half.'

'He had been dead *over* an hour?' Storm inserted sharply. 'And what time did you find him?'

'It couldn't have been later than six-fifteen, perhaps a few minutes before,' Shore said intensely. He waited for some response from Storm. The detective gestured impatiently.

'Naturally, I was stunned,' the doctor said. 'I first looked at the wound. I tested for any reflexes. And then . . . it was then that I saw the scrap of woolen cloth in Payne's left hand. Instantly I recognized the thin pin-stripe running through it! It was a scrap of material from a suit of mine! I knew, Storm! I was as positive as any man can be! I . . . I stared about the room. In the ashtray on the desk was a cigar — it was neatly balanced on the edge with a long ash hanging to the end! I began to think, to realize: Someone had telephoned me, called me to this house!

That unknown person had posed as Payne, but Payne had been dead at five o'clock — at the time the call was made! I was certain of that. And now . . . here was a scrap torn from a suit of mine, hanging in the fingers of a murdered man! I . . . can't you see?' he demanded harshly. 'I knew! I was certain! And I thought of what had happened two days before.'

'What was that?' Storm asked intently.

'I'd been searching for stamps at my apartment. As I was looking through the drawers of a little writing desk I have in my room, I'd run across a memorandum; it was written on my paper, written in a handwriting that was startlingly like my own! But I'd never written, never even seen, the memo before.'

'What was the nature of this memo?'

'It didn't say so outright, but I knew instantly that it concerned Gregory Payne's will. It was brief. It was: 'To Linda, seven-eighths; to Goode, Gabriel, Darby, and Shore, each one-fourth of the one-eighth remaining. If no Linda and no heirs or issues, total to be divided equally between Goode, Gabriel, Darby, and

Shore.' That was all it said. But I knew at once what it was,' Shore went on swiftly. 'I knew it was a forgery. It had no place in my desk. I . . . I destroyed it at once, mentioned it to no one. But . . . but that afternoon when I found Payne's body, when I found the scrap of my suit in his fingers, and when I realized that someone had called me there, I thought instantly of the memo. It was all inexplicable. But I saw the pattern. Someone had murdered Payne, and wished me to appear to be the killer. The note had been intended for police consumption — they were to find it!'

'And what did you do, Shore?' Storm asked carefully.

'I thought of calling the police and telling the truth. But it was mad! How could I expect them to believe me? I might remove the cloth from Payne's hand, but what other evidence was there that pointed to me? Evidence I did not see, knew nothing about? I couldn't take the chance — it was gambling my life against the credulity of men who aren't usually credulous! I realized I must destroy the evidence I knew about that pointed to me; I must make other evidence in its place, and I must cover my own tracks as best I could. I . . . I had to act fast. I studied the wound in the temple. Suicide! I would make it look like suicide!' He gestured. He swallowed and mopped his perspiring face again.

'I looked about the room carefully. On the table beside the hall door, I found a pistol. It was Payne's, I realized. It still bore the odor of recent fire; one shot was missing. I decided that I would have to take one big chance — I would have to gamble that Payne had been killed with his own gun. I needed a motive for suicide, then. I searched through his desk. Fortunately . . . ' Shore began, then caught himself. 'Anyway, I found an envelope from my office, postmarked a week previously, and containing a bill. I destroyed the bill and wrote a short letter to Payne in longhand. I told him I doubted that he was as ill as he thought he was. I suggested that his entire trouble was the mental depression and melancholy of which he had spoken to me. I advised him to come into New York and place himself under the care of a psychiatrist. I offered to arrange a first appointment. In closing, I assured him that I had followed his wishes and mentioned his difficulty and melancholy to no one. Then . . . I placed that letter in the postmarked envelope, and placed the envelope in his desk.' He stopped, coughed heavily, fingered his pockets nervously. Storm tossed him the pack of cigarettes and matches. Linda saw his fingers shaking violently as he cupped the flame and lit the cigarette. He breathed haltingly and continued:

'I went downstairs to my car and got my pistol from the dashboard compartment. I returned to Payne's room. I took the volume of the Encyclopedia from the bookcase and opened it on the bed. I placed my gun in Payne's right hand. With my own hand I forced his hand to grip the gun. I fired one shot into the pages of the book. You see, I've done some work for the police. I knew of the dermal-nitrate test that's used to determine whether a hand has recently fired a gun. A cast is made of the back of the hand. When it is pulled away, it draws particles of gunpowder from the hand, if the hand has recently fired a gun. I was trying to establish proof that Payne had fired a gun. Then I removed my gun, wiped all prints from Payne's gun, and placed it in his hand. I removed the scrap of cloth from his left hand. I took the cigar from the ashtray — I wanted nothing to suggest that it hadn't been suicide. I wiped the doorknobs as I left the house. I took with me the volume in which was buried the bullet from my gun. I went straight home. I used the emergency stairs to reach my apartment. I looked in my closet; there was my blue suit with the pin stripe. And the scrap that had been in Payne's hand fitted exactly into a torn place of one sleeve! It was from my suit, just as I'd known! I . . . I ripped the pages from the book and burned them. The smoke caused the manager to come up. I didn't get time to burn the stiff back of the book. I intended to throw it away, and . . . and then you found it, I suppose. I . . . When my wife came home, I told her everything. We decided to tell everyone that we had been in the apartment alone together since about five that afternoon. And that . . . that is the truth, Storm,' Shore said in raw sincerity. 'I swear to God I didn't kill Payne! Everything I did, however questionable and incriminating, was done to clear myself of a crime I didn't commit!'

'And I assume you carried through on your suicide story when the police questioned you after the body was found?'

'I did, but . . . Oh, God, you can't imagine the agony of lying when you . . . when you don't know whether the police have proof that destroys everything you are telling. I told them, yes. I told them that Payne had imagined he was losing his mind. I told them he had spoken to me in utter confidence. I . . . I suppose they believed me. They had found my letter in his desk.'

'I see,' Storm mused distantly. 'And are you going to tell me that the missing bullet of your gun was the one you fired into the Encyclopedia that day?'

'No. I cleaned my gun carefully that night and filled the cylinder. The next morning I returned it to my car. I . . . since that day I've paid no attention to the gun until I noticed it yesterday. I opened the compartment to get my sunglasses out; I was starting out here. I found the gun at the front of the compartment. I usually keep it pushed down behind gloves and papers at the back. I glanced at it as I pushed it back. I saw that one shell was missing. I was puzzled, but I gave it little thought. I mean, I gave it little thought until you brought out the fact that someone had attempted to kill Linda at ten o'clock Saturday evening. The instant you mentioned that, I was sick with fear. I realized that, once again, I'd been drawn out here on a fake call at a time when murder had been attempted — a murder which would have affected a will in which I was an interested party. And a shot was inexplicably missing from my gun! I . . . Think, man! What would have been your reaction under those circumstances? What would you have done, knowing what had transpired, on the day of Payne's death! You would have been frantic to dispose of that gun! *Wouldn't* you?' he demanded harshly.

Storm smiled without humor. 'Perhaps. And so you waited until Walter Gordon was asleep, then you slipped from the room, took the gun from the car, and threw it in the creek. Whereupon Reddy accosted you . . . '

'Yes, I did that,' the doctor admitted heavily. 'I didn't know I was being followed. I . . . I was just trying to save myself.' His eyes hung beseechingly on Storm's face. 'You believe me, don't you?' he breathed. 'You see how it was, don't you? You know I wouldn't have told all this if . . . if I had killed Payne! You *must* know that, man!' he exclaimed in a whisper.

'I'll reserve my answer for a while,' Storm suggested with a note of irony. 'We are going to hear about the relationship of Glenn Darby and Mr. Coke Brill — the angry gentleman over there.' He pointed to the heavy-bodied, well-dressed man, then looked steadily at Glenn Darby.

'In order that you will feel safe in talking freely, I assure you that I know all about the body at the well, Darby. I know that you were aware of that body. But I also know that you did not kill that woman. In the first place, you don't have the courage to murder. You need have no fear in talking; the body is gone. It was destroyed in the burning of your house.'

'It was ... You mean — ' Darby breathed.

'Keep your mouth shut, you damned idiot!' Brill said softly. 'Don't you know a lie when you hear one?'

'Am I lying, Darby,' Storm asked with heavy surprise, 'when I tell you I know you stole Payne's will from this room three months ago? And am I lying when I tell you I know that Brill ordered you into New York last Saturday night, ordered you to have that fixed fight? Am I lying when I say he told you to save carefully the evidence on that cameo ring?'

'You know ... all of that?' the blond man breathed thinly.

'And I'm going to know everything else. If you want to save your own hide, you can start talking now.'

'Tell him, Glenn!' Karen cried. 'You've got to tell it! Tell it now and get it all over with, for God's sake!'

From the depths of his chest, Coke Brill loosened a tide of raw whispered obscenity. His hot eyes rested on Karen's pale face. Then he spun to face Storm.

'And who in hell's going to listen to her?' he asked acidly. 'What is she? I'll tell you what she is! Look in her purse. Open one of those little lipstick containers she keeps! You — '

'Shut up! Shut up!' Karen screamed wildly. She jerked from her chair, her eyes aflame with fury. Reddy broke forward and grasped her as she lunged toward the man. He held her as she writhed and fought against his grip. Brill laughed metallically.

'Watch her! She's playing it honest now! But open those lipsticks and you won't find any lipstick! You'll find heroin! She's nothing but a dope, a dreamy, a damned hophead! That's all she ever was, and it's all she ever will be! It — '

Karen choked. Storm pounded the desk.

'Sit down, Brill! Shut up! Sit down, damn you! I — '

'Maybe the blond guy thinks she's a new angel?' Brill tore out sarcastically. 'She's been in more beds than a traveling — '

Storm moved two feet. His left arm lashed out. Linda saw Brill's head snap backward. The sodden smacking sound echoed through the room. Brill staggered backward and hit his chair. He caught himself and swayed there in silence. A drop of blood slid down from his lips and fell off his chin. His pale eyes glazed with an animal fury.

11

Storm watched Brill sit down. He looked at Karen. She was utterly motionless in Reddy's grasp. Her face was dead-white, her eyes dark and listless.

'Let her go,' Storm said quietly. 'Sit down, Karen.'

She obeyed mutely. Storm returned to his chair behind the desk. He looked at Darby.

'I'm ready for you to start talking.'

The blond man stared vacantly at Storm. He swallowed and wet his lips. 'What . . . do you want me to say?' he asked thickly.

'Why did Brill order you to go into New York last Saturday night?'

'I . . . didn't . . . don't know,' Darby whispered. 'He didn't tell me. I swear he didn't tell me.'

'But why did you have to do as he ordered?'

'Because . . . ' Darby swallowed again. 'I borrowed some money from him. I

'. . . I just borrowed some money.'

'When? How much?' Storm snapped impatiently.

'It was five thousand dollars. He loaned it to me about three months ago.'

'Three months ago, when a will was stolen . . . ' Linda saw a sudden bleak gleam flicker in the detective's eyes. 'Just how did you happen to get that much money from Brill? What security could you offer to cover five thousand dollars, Darby?'

'I didn't have any . . . any real security,' Glenn stammered.

'You didn't get five thousand from Brill on your promise!'

'Tell him the truth, Glenn!' Karen cried. 'He's going to find out. Tell him now.'

'I just showed him the will — showed him how I'd get some money from Uncle Gregory when he died,' Glenn explained uneasily.

'Brill loaned you the money on the basis of Payne's will?'

'He . . . Yes. At first he didn't, but then he changed his mind.'

'Tell me about it,' Storm said patiently. 'Go on.'

'But that's all there was to it,' Glenn Darby said harshly. 'I needed some money. I saw the will on the table over there. I got it . . . just borrowed it,' he explained haltingly. 'I took it to Brill. I knew he always carried lots of money. I asked for a loan. I showed him how I'd be able to pay him back some day. I offered to pay him double whatever he loaned me. First he said no. Then . . . well, he took the will and read it. He said he'd think about it. The next day he came over to my house and gave me the five thousand dollars. I signed a note. That . . . that's all there was to it,' he said, breathing heavily.

Storm turned to look at Karen. Her dark eyes were fixed on Darby, as though mutely striving to drag words from his lips. Storm faced Darby again.

'That's not all,' he snapped. 'If you don't tell the whole truth, I think Karen will. Which is it going to be?'

Darby swallowed drily. 'I don't understand the rest . . . Brill came to see me a few times after he loaned me the money. Then he . . . one day he said it was due

— that was about a month ago. I told him he was wrong; I said there hadn't been any time limit, but he showed me the note I'd signed. And he'd made it for sixty days. I . . . I tried to argue with him. He wouldn't listen. He kept saying he'd have to take the note to Uncle Gregory and show him how I'd borrowed against his death. I knew Uncle Gregory would be furious. He'd cut me out of his will. I told Brill that, and he just . . . he just grinned and said, 'And you'll still owe me, and I always get my money.' I . . . I asked him what I could do. Finally, he said he'd let the whole thing drop if I'd sign over my entire part of Uncle Gregory's estate to him. If I didn't, he'd tell Uncle Gregory. I . . . I had to sign.'

'So, for five thousand dollars, you sold your rights to anything you might receive from Payne's estate,' Storm summarized carefully. 'And then what happened?'

'Then . . . it was hardly a week later that he started coming to my house every night. Every night he'd come there and talk. He'd talk about everything — ask questions about everything,' Darby explained jerkily. Now his words came tumbling across his lips like a suddenly released wave.

'He'd bring me a bottle of whiskey almost every time. We'd drink a little. He'd ask me about Uncle Gregory — about his habits and when he was at home; he'd ask me when Goode was usually gone from here, and where Linda went and when. He started asking questions about Shore and Gabriel, too. About where they lived and who they lived with and how often they came out to see Uncle Gregory. He asked if they had much money, and if they ever carried a gun, and if — '

'What was your answer to that?' Storm interrupted.

'About the gun?' Darby frowned uncertainly. 'I guess I told him about Shore's gun. I'd seen it once in the car when Shore gave me a ride into New York.'

The doctor choked furiously and twisted to glare at Brill. The pale-eyed man had eyes for no one but Darby. He watched without moving a muscle, without seeming to draw a breath.

'Go on, Darby,' Storm ordered.

'Well, I . . . I never understood him, but I was afraid — of Brill and the way he was acting. I knew he was thinking, planning something, but I didn't know what. And that went on until a Saturday, two weeks ago. Then . . . one night, it . . . it happened,' he whispered tightly.

Linda found herself on the edge of her chair. In the corner of her eye, she saw Brill's white fingers slowly clenching until they were gnarled balls of flesh and bone.

'Yes? And what was it that happened, Darby?' Storm prompted.

'Brill was there again. There was some gin. I . . . I was drinking. Drunk, I guess,' he panted heavily. 'I can't remember much. It's all tangled, like a crazy dream. It was night. I was drinking and Brill was talking, grinning at me, and his pale eyes were watching me, and . . . And I don't remember another damned thing! I swear to God, Storm, I don't remember another damned thing until . . . until I saw the body,' he breathed.

Storm's eyes held Darby in a relentless grip. Darby's words plunged on in swift tumult:

'I . . . me and Brill . . . we were down in the grove of trees where the farmhouse used to be. Brill was cursing at me, whispering at me to help him before somebody found us. And he was rolling rocks and pushing dirt down in the old well-hole. There was a woman down there — a woman's body with the head all smashed and bloody. She was dead!' Darby cried. He gestured wildly.

'I didn't understand . . . couldn't remember . . . couldn't think! I guess I did what Brill told me. We covered the body and packed the dirt. We went back to my house. And there . . . there on the floor was the poker to my fireplace. There was blood on it — blood all over it. And when I saw my hands in the light, there was blood all over them. I . . . I started trying to ask Brill what had happened. He cursed me and told me to stop acting like a damned idiot. He said I'd killed the woman myself, and I knew it damned well. But . . . but I didn't. I couldn't remember anything, Storm. I swear I couldn't. I . . . He made me clean my hands. He straightened up the room. I kept begging him to tell me. Finally, he said the woman had come to the door and asked how to get to Warburn. He said I'd been drunk, walking up and down the room, raving about how much money I used to have and how I'd never got a break and how I hated the world's guts and all that. I'd cursed the woman and told her to get out. Then I'd hit her, he said; hit her with the poker. I'd tried to choke her. I'd said something about 'the fools thrive while the genius must steal.' Then he'd pulled me off, but it was too late. She was dead. We'd taken her down to the well, and . . . and that was where I started remembering again.' Darby stopped to swallow rawly. 'But I didn't remember it. I didn't want . . . think of killing her. I swear I didn't know about it — nothing about it!'

'Then why did you swallow the story?' Storm demanded.

'I . . . Because I *could* remember it, too. I mean . . . You can't understand, but . . . I have felt that way — wanted to hit, to choke people. Lots of times when I get drunk, I think about it . . . kind of halfway a dream. They can sweep a street and make money ... sell papers and make money ... and I write and I never make a dime. And that ... that's where those words come in — those words about 'the fools thrive while the genius must steal ... '' Darby stared pleadingly at Storm. 'I can remember saying them — just those words. That's all I can remember, I swear. About the poker and the blood on my hands or the woman coming to the door ... I can't remember that at all!'

'Let me get this,' Storm said slowly. 'You don't remember the actual murdering of the woman, but you recall what you said to her? Is that it?'

'No, I ... Not to her! I ... Oh, I can't explain!'

'He just remembers imagining all of that somewhere, but not there,' Karen explained frantically.

'Wait!' Linda said sharply. 'Those words about the fools thriving ... I've heard them, too! You wrote them, Glenn! They were in a story you let me read one time.'

Storm looked at her quickly. 'You're positive?'

'Positive.'

Storm looked back toward Darby. 'Go on. And then what?'

'I . . . I was crazy with fear. I didn't know what to do. Brill told me to do nothing. Leave the body absolutely alone, he said. Don't go around the grave. Don't move the body. He said he'd keep his mouth shut about me murdering the woman if I'd leave the body alone. But if I tried to move it, he said, I'd be playing with fire; I could get him tangled in. If I started that, he swore he'd tell the whole story to the police. And, just to keep me honest, he said, he was taking the bloodstained poker with my fingerprints on it. If I cheeped, the police would get the proof.'

'Naturally,' Storm agreed drily. 'And what came next?'

'It . . . He . . . Every night he came back to my house. He'd question me about what I'd done — if I'd been near the body. He told me to keep quiet about knowing him. That went on until . . . until

Saturday a week ago . . . the thirteenth. That day he came out to my house. It was in the afternoon, about four o'clock when he got there.' Darby mopped at his face and his tongue roamed thickly along his lips.

'He told me to get dressed, that I was going to New York and meet Karen. He said she'd be waiting for me at Grand Central Station. I . . . I started asking questions. He bit me off every time. He acted nervous, in a hurry — different from any way I'd ever seen him. He kept pushing me to hurry, to get dressed. He gave me a ride to the edge of Warburn and told me to get the four-thirty train and stay in New York until after eleven o'clock. And last, he said if I opened my mouth a little bit about him or anything he'd been doing, I'd be stuck with the murder of that woman. Then he left me and drove back the way he'd come. I . . . I went to New York like he said, and stayed there with Karen until almost midnight. I went . . . came back out here. The next day, I heard that Uncle Gregory had killed himself.'

'But you *knew* Brill had murdered him?' Storm demanded harshly. 'You *knew* that! Answer me! Didn't you?'

'No . . . Yes . . . I . . . ' Darby choked. 'I mean, at first I believed what the papers and police said — about it being suicide. But then, in a couple of days, Brill started coming back. He wanted to know what was going on. He said he'd heard that a private dick was on the case. He almost . . . one day he almost strangled me. He said I'd talked. I swore I hadn't talked about anything. He wanted to know what was holding up the splitting of the estate. Then . . . then I began to know . . . to know for sure. I was . . . Oh, God, I was frightened! I wanted to tell, to get away from Brill. But I couldn't. He knew about the woman — the grave. He had the poker. And I knew he'd kill me, too. I *knew* he would. I . . . I couldn't think of anything. I . . . And then . . . last Saturday evening,' Darby said heavily and harshly, 'I saw a light over here. I came over. It was Linda. She was back.' For an instant his eyes slid toward Linda. She looked into their tortured depth. And then she closed her eyes. She heard Glenn's anxious voice stumbling on:

'I was afraid for her. I didn't want her to stay here — anywhere around where Brill was. I . . . See, I'd read the will again, and all of a sudden I realized what would happen if she died too. Brill would get a lot more. I knew he'd do it. I was frantic when I found her here that night.'

'And what did you do?' Storm asked ironically.

Darby stared at him. 'I couldn't do anything. If I had . . . Brill would have killed me. I knew that,' he whimpered again.

Linda glanced up as she heard Walt curse very softly.

'I went back home,' Darby resumed. 'Brill was there when I got there. Another man, a man I'd never seen, was there too. Each of them had a car. Brill had a gun. He told me I was going to ride into New York with the stranger. He said I'd drive. That I'd go to Thirty-Second Street near Fifth Avenue. At ten o'clock a man would appear. I was to hand this man my cameo ring. When the man gave it back, I was to

213

put it in a little box Brill gave me and keep it. He said I'd need it to save my neck. And, finally, he said I'd keep my mouth shut or I'd never be able to prove I'd been in New York at ten. And, on top of that, the police would find the woman's body. And they would find me . . . dead.' Darby gestured wildly. 'That's what he said. He said if I made one bad move or opened my mouth about him, I'd be killed. Then he sent me into New York with the stranger. He didn't go with us. At the place on Thirty-Second, the man showed up and took my ring. He raked it across his temple at the hairline, then handed it back. 'You've just had your fight,' he said. 'If you're good, I'll show up when you need me and prove it. If you're not, try to make the cops believe you.' Then he disappeared. The first stranger drove me back to a place near my house and let me out. And then . . . that was all. The next morning, you came over and I told you about the ring and the fight. And that's all,' Darby panted. 'It's the truth — everything!'

When the hot words ended, a strange,

stagnant silence fell upon the room. Linda's eyes, with the eyes of all the others, fixed themselves on the flabby, gray-white face of Coke Brill. *The man who killed my father*, Linda thought, and she felt her nails dig into the flesh of her palms.

'So that's the story,' Storm said, his voice flat and metallic. He paused. For a moment his eyes, filled with deep contempt, lingered on Darby's face, then he turned to Brill. 'You were shrewd enough, Brill, in your estimate of Darby. You knew you were dealing with a drunk, an unbalanced coward. You knew he hadn't the courage to make the slightest move against you, nor the wisdom to penetrate the fraud of the woman's murder. You knew he would wait, obeying every order you gave him, until the estate was divided, until you had taken your share. Then you would kill him.'

'And you've got it all figured out?' Brill said drily.

Storm went on deliberately: 'You realized the potentialities of the will when Darby brought it to you. Then and there you began to plot the deaths of Gregory Payne and Linda Payne. You questioned Darby concerning the habits of Payne, of Goode, of Linda. You asked about Gabriel and Shore. Why . . . ? Because you wanted a fall guy for the murder. It couldn't be Darby; he had to be innocent to inherit. But someone else would serve a double purpose: First, to complete the murder picture; second, to increase the amount of money which would go to Darby. Say Shore had been convicted of the murder, as you planned, then his share would probably have been divided, giving Darby more. And then, while you planned your crimes, the woman appeared.'

'Yeah,' Brill grunted sarcastically. 'Tell me about her.'

'She knew you. She learned what you planned to do. She came to Payne to warn him. You heard of this in some way, then traced her to the Sequin Arms. You managed to find out that she planned to visit Payne again on that Saturday night. Again, a double purpose shows itself . . . You would murder her to eliminate risk to your plan, and in her death you would gain a club to swing over Darby's head . . . So you got Darby drunk, left him at his house when the time came, slipped over to this house, and killed the woman as she came up the driveway. You took the body to the well-hole and half-buried it. You stained Darby's hands with her blood. You had used his poker to kill her. Then you carried Darby to the hole. When he regained consciousness after passing out, you told him the murder tale.'

Brill blinked and edged forward on his chair. He blinked without any trace of emotion. 'How much of all this do you think you can prove?' he asked quietly.

'You're being optimistic,' Storm said ironically. 'If I know anything about juries, you'll be the proverbial snowball in hell. We would start with a subtle review of your criminal record, involving bootlegging and tainted with dope. We would hear Darby's story. Perhaps Karen can add something. But if you demand proof, I think I can get it, Brill.'

'How?'

'The man with whom Darby had the

'fight.' I think I can find him. I have a feeling that when he hears of your present situation, he may see the wisdom of changing sides.'

'And you think you can find him?' Brill murmured softly. His pale eyes were estimating Storm's face.

'Yes. I think I know what happened that night. You wanted the fight to be questionable, so absurd that Darby would look like a fool when he told of it — if he ever had to. And yet you wanted to be able to convince the law that such a fight, no matter how fantastic it sounded, had actually happened. Thus the flesh and blood and hair on the ring which Darby was instructed to save. When the time came, you would produce the man to fit those hairs, a man to satisfy the chemical tests upon the hair and blood and flesh. But would that be enough . . . ? I have a feeling you went one step further, Brill. I think you wanted it positively known that the fake fight with that certain man happened at ten o'clock. So . . . I think that if I checked every doctor within a two-block radius of Thirty-Second Street and Fifth Avenue, I'd find one who treated a man last Saturday night for a scalp cut — and treated him at a few minutes after ten. That doctor will be able to describe the man he treated. I'll be able to locate him. And he will be made to talk.' Storm paused and cocked a brow. 'I wonder if I'm right?' he mused gently.

Slowly Brill pushed himself from his chair. 'I'm not what you'd call a plain damned fool, Storm. I know a little law. I know this, for instance: You can tag me for concealing that murder over there in the well — maybe. If you get the right jury, maybe you could ride me in for attempted murder. You could give me a ragged ride, sure,' he admitted quietly. 'Maybe I'm due a little: I never should have trusted little Karen, the bitch! I'll tell you this,' he finished flatly, 'I don't think you're going to do any of those things.'

Linda stared at the man's cold face. She could not believe her ears. Storm's lips twitched.

'No?' he mocked. 'And why not?'

'Because we're going to make a trade. We're going to have a talk. When we get through, you're going to call yourself a damned fool. You'll trade me cheap for what I'll give you.'

'I doubt it,' Storm said bleakly.

Brill laughed harshly and gestured. 'Get 'em out of here! We'll see how fast you change your mind. Get 'em all out of here!'

Storm frowned. Abruptly, he gestured to Reddy. 'Everybody out,' he ordered. 'No one leave the house until — '

'And you can keep the lady in here.' Brill jerked a finger toward Linda. 'I want it fixed so you won't forget. It's her party, anyway,' he added, with a brittle, ugly laugh.

12

The hall door closed behind Reddy, and Linda was left in the study with Storm and Brill. The room was close and hot. Brill pulled a chair deliberately toward the desk. He sat down and lit a cigar. All the while Storm watched him relentlessly.

'It's a funny damned thing, a woman,' Brill mused in his bass voice. 'I'd never have picked her to fall for a punk like Darby. But maybe I'm getting old,' he said, looking down at his paunch. 'But that's that,' he said. He shifted himself and gazed steadily at Storm.

'For a guy that hasn't killed anybody, that's a nice setup you laid against me,' he said agreeably. 'You're making me tear up a perfect playhouse to get loose.'

'But you feel that you'll get loose?'

'Oh, yes. After a fashion, that is. It'll be asking a little too much to figure on nothing. I'd guess about three to five years. With your help.' He settled his huge body comfortably in the chair.

'You won't get it.'

'On the contrary, I think I will,' Brill countered. 'You see, Storm, I did *not* kill that woman. I never saw her before in my life until I saw her dead. Furthermore, I walked into this house on the thirteenth to kill Payne, and I found *him* dead. I did *not* kill him. But I know who did,' he said very quietly. 'I not only know, but I can prove it beyond anybody's last doubt. As I said, I'm no fool. I have the evidence. In fact, it was going to make very nice blackmail before you came along. But now . . . ' He shrugged.

'And who did kill Payne and the woman?' Storm asked.

'Oh, not so fast. We haven't traded yet. Let me point out the advantages of my information.' He leaned back and held up one finger.

'First,' Brill said, 'I have been following your motions. From what I know, and from what I've seen and heard here tonight, the real killer has done a nice job of blanketing himself. I can say almost positively that you're not going to get him, Storm. And I'm not bluffing. Second, he is planning to kill the lady here.' He nodded to Linda. 'I know that. So what happens if you don't give me a break? If you ring me up, you kill her; not tonight or tomorrow, maybe, but you kill her just like you held the gun. On the other hand — you promise me a soft touch in court, I tell you all I know and give you proof — proof I couldn't possibly have framed . . . Then you've got the murderer of Payne and the woman, and in addition you've saved the lady's life. Think about it,' he said shrewdly. 'That way, you get plenty. You lose a big rap on me, but what am I? You say I'm a criminal. Okay. You're trading a criminal a few years for the life of her here; plus a double killer in the bargain.' He paused. 'Do you want it?'

Storm studied Brill's face for a full minute.

'I won't trade in the dark. And if I agree to anything, it binds nobody but me. You'll have to tell me more, and you'll have to take your chances beyond me.'

'But you're ready to listen,' Brill

murmured softly. 'All I'll want is a toning-down on the shot at the lady. You plush me there, and say I helped reveal the killer. You say that on the stand.'

'I haven't promised anything,' Storm said bleakly. 'I'm waiting to hear you talk.'

'Okay. Like I said, the woman was dead and in that hole when I first saw her. Payne was dead when I found him in his room about five-twenty on the thirteenth. But this is the way it went . . . I was over at Darby's the night the woman was killed. He was drunk. In fact, he passed out. I was leaving. I went in the bathroom, but I didn't turn the light on. I was there when I heard footsteps passing outside the window. I looked out. A man was looking into the front-room window at Darby, stretched out on the floor. The man stood there watching Darby for about three minutes, like he was making certain Darby was out for a good stretch. All this time the man didn't see me; he didn't see my car. It was parked about fifty feet from the house, and it was dark that night. There was nothing in the room to tell anybody I was there unless he saw me in person. The man never knew. He slipped away from the house and headed down toward the creek — not along the trail that leads over here, but across the field. I was curious, naturally. I didn't trust Darby completely. I wanted to know where this man fitted. So I followed him.'

'To the grave?'

'To the grave in the clump of trees. He worked mostly in the dark, but he used a small flashlight once — when he was working with a knife, doing something. He dragged some clothes off the body and finally he buried it. When he got through, I heard him heading off at an angle, going toward the lane over by Darby's house. I kept following him. Once, a car passed, and I saw him fall into a ditch: he was carrying a bundle under his arm. He wasn't going toward Warburn, but heading toward Hamond-ville, three miles up from here. When he got to a vacant filling station about a mile outside of Hamondville, he crawled through the high restroom window. Ten minutes later he came out. He didn't have the bundle anymore. He was heading into

Hamondville fast. I started to follow. When I passed the filling station, I saw a faint red glow inside at the back. I knew it was a fire. And when you have a fire after a murder, Storm, you're losing evidence. I worked my way through a front window and found the fire. It was in the bottom of an empty oil drum. I dumped the drum over and snagged the burning stuff out with a stick. I beat out the fire and looked at what I had. They were clothes — wet and muddy and bloody clothes and shoes; a woman's brassiere, and part of a slip; a woman's cloth purse with a little junk inside. A — '

'The wet and muddy clothes were those of a man?' Storm interrupted suddenly.

'Yeah. So I wrapped the stuff up and went back to Darby's. He was starting to groan and stir around a little. I hid the stuff in my car. I decided I'd get my axe on Darby while I had the chance. I lugged him down to the grave and uncovered the body some. I messed up his hands and his poker with blood. When he came around, I fed him the story. He'd babbled to me a couple of times about how he hated people and how he'd choke one someday. Then I spotted that line about the stupid thriving . . . It was typed out on a sheet of paper on his desk.' Brill stirred and flicked the ash from his cigar.

'Well, I went on into New York, and looked over the stuff I'd salvaged from the fire. I found out who the woman had been from her purse, and what had been the matter with her — '

'What had been the matter with her?' Storm asked sharply.

Brill smiled drily. 'You get that information the minute you tell me we've traded. I'm just . . . kind of breaking down your sales resistance now.' He winked infuriatingly and tapped his cigar again. 'By cautious inquiry, as you might call it, I doped out how the man at the window fitted with her. I was ready,' he said comfortably. 'At least until tonight,' he added, with a rueful smile. 'I hid my evidence in a good place. A very good place, Storm, so don't waste your time trying to short-circuit me.'

Again he paused to study Storm,

judging the detective's mood. At last, he continued lazily:

'The afternoon arrived — the thirteenth. I had planned to take care of Payne that afternoon. I sent Darby into New York to be with Karen. At that time I was, unfortunately, of the opinion that she could be trusted. Our relationship was intimate at that time, to put it neatly. I got over here. I was ready to take care of Goode without any trouble, but he wasn't around. I prowled upstairs, and what did I find? Not Payne, but his body. And it may be funny, after what Shore told you, but there was his gun in his hand, just like he'd killed himself.'

Storm jerked forward. 'He held the gun in . . . No! You don't expect me to swallow all this!' he said angrily.

'I'm not asking you to swallow anything, Storm,' Brill said comfortably. 'I'm just giving you the facts. With the information I've got, you can prove what I'm telling you. But, anyway, I knew immediately who had killed Payne. Here it was, set up to look like a suicide. I could leave it that way and run the chance that the cops would believe it, or I could go ahead like I'd intended and frame Shore. I decided to frame Shore; I wanted to leave the real killer for a little blackmail treatment later on, and I knew that maybe he'd left some loose ends. So I took the gun out of Payne's hand. I put the scrap of cloth from Shore's suit in his left hand, like Payne had fought with him and torn the suit. I'd lifted a few strands of Shore's hair from the comb in Shore's bathroom. I was going to plant them. I had a fingerprinted heavy letter-opener from Shore's desk that I was going to use for the job. I didn't plan to shoot Payne — scared of the noise, you see. But before I got everything fixed, I heard a car arriving. I took a look. I'd called Shore to come out. I intended to slug him and leave him there, tipping the cops to investigate. But it wasn't Shore's car. All of a sudden I realized that maybe somebody had heard the shot that *had* killed Payne, and this was the real stuff. I couldn't wait to be sure. I beat it, locked the doors, and crossed the creek to my car, which was over near Darby's place.'

'And that would have been Gabriel arriving,' Storm mused. 'Did you place a phone call to him?'

'No. My only call was to Shore. But that's all I've done, Storm. I just found the body of the woman after she'd been killed. I found Payne's body after he'd been killed. Therefore, I haven't committed any crime yet, have I?'

'You attempted to murder Mrs. Gordon,' Storm reminded.

'Yes. That's my one error, I guess you'd say,' Brill confessed genially. 'I'd been calling on the phone to see if she'd come back here. Saturday night, early, I called again. The flunky answered. I guess she remembers.' He glanced at Linda.

She found herself nodding fixedly.

'So I came out, first dropping by for Shore's gun. I gave him a ring to come out this way. You see, I still thought he was under suspicion regarding Payne's death. But, anyway,' Brill said with a touch of irony, 'you know all that's worth knowing now. It's the truth. Like I've said, you can help me on a soft rap and I'll help you plenty. And what I'm selling you is worth the price, Storm.' He leaned back and licked his thick lips. 'What do you say?'

Linda looked at Storm. His keen eyes were dark and furious. He chewed his lower lip as he studied Brill's face. He mashed out his cigarette and rose abruptly.

'Why in hell should I believe you?' he demanded scornfully. 'You could frame any proof you handed me — '

'No, Storm. The kind of stuff I've got on the woman can't be framed or faked by anybody in the world. I swear that. It just can't be framed. And when you've got it, you've got the killer in your glove.' He smiled, watching Storm with an expression of baited amusement.

'Hey! Get the water!' a voice shouted excitedly from across the hall. 'Get the water before the whole house catches on — '

Running feet churned down the hall. Doors slammed violently. Other voices rose in a crescendo of excitement. Linda started toward the hall door. Storm was there before her. 'What the devil — ' he began.

His words were never finished. Through

the study smashed the blasting thunder of a gun. In the wake of its fury came one thick, hushed choke of agony.

Linda and Storm turned frantically. In one shattered instant Linda's eyes caught the blank, stunned expression on the face of Coke Brill. He was standing utterly still in the center of the room. As she watched she saw a thin, fast river of darkness come spilling from his temple. She heard Storm curse in insane fury. She saw Brill falling, saw his pale eyes rolling upward.

Then the entire scene was blacked out as the house was plunged into darkness. Throughout the house broke wild turmoil as voices screamed, as furniture crashed and shattered, as feet thundered over the floors.

'Lie down! *Down*, Linda!' Storm raged. His steps plunged toward the hall door.

'Get the lights on!' Gabriel's frantic bass wailed from some distant room.

'Stand where you are! Everybody stand still!' Reddy shouted.

'I've got the light switch!' Walt shouted. 'Here . . . Hell! The fuses are burned out!'

Storm's running steps faded toward the rear of the house, and Linda was left alone on the floor of the dark study. She lay there, too shocked and frightened to breathe. And as she lay, she felt — as surely and vividly, as if by touch — the body of Coke Brill near her in the darkness.

13

It seemed to Linda that an eternity of nightmare passed, but it was no more than three minutes before the lights blazed on. Out in the hall, the hubbub of frantic voices came to life.

Doors slammed. Steps hurried back along the hall, and Storm appeared in the doorway. He looked at Linda, glanced on toward the body of Brill, and then turned.

'Take them all in the living room, Reddy,' he ordered, in a voice ragged with tense fury. 'Search everyone. You, Elsie, help him. Get in that living room, all of you!'

Linda heard no more words. Slow scuffing footsteps came to her from the hall. Storm closed and locked the door.

'You can get up,' he said more quietly to her. 'Stay here until I can leave with you.'

She rose, trembling. A cold hard ball seemed to hover in the pit of her stomach. Almost as if hypnotized, her unwilling eyes followed the slender figure of the detective as he knelt over the fat body of Brill.

She saw him move the eyelids, turn the head slightly. He straightened and stared around the room. The French doors were closed and the drapes drawn. He crossed the room quickly to the door that led from the study to the downstairs bathroom. He turned the knob and entered the small room. Linda heard the light switch snapping; it snapped again. Storm cursed softly. She heard a key grating in the door that opened from the bathroom into the hall. Storm returned. He hesitated one final moment as his eyes raked the room impatiently. He pulled the cloth from the table and threw it over the body, then turned to Linda.

'Let's go across,' he said. His voice was suddenly weary. She nodded mutely. She followed him from the room and he locked the hall door of the study. Together they entered the living room.

Linda stopped. The room was heavy with smoke. Someone was coughing. The odor of burned cloth reached her nostrils. Then, through the thinning haze of smoke, she saw the huge black smoke-stain that covered the wall beside the front window. She saw the heavy drapery-rod hanging askew across the top of the window. The drapes were gone.

'Nothing there,' Reddy was muttering monotonously. She turned. Shore, Gabriel, and the rest of them stood in a line against the wall. At the moment, Goode stood forward out of the line, and Reddy's hands were moving in and out of the man's pockets.

Walt's eyes met hers and he smiled uneasily. Water stained his pants and formed a pool about his feet.

'You next,' Reddy said snappishly.

Walt jerked his eyes from Linda and stepped forward out of the line.

Linda looked at Storm. He was surveying the room. He said nothing until Reddy completed the search.

'Find anything?' he asked drily.

'Nothing.'

'Then search the house. I want a gun that's been fired recently. Look all through the house. Look outside. It could have been thrown out. Help him, Elsie. The rest of you, sit down,' he added irritably. 'Wait. Before you go, Reddy: what about that?' He jerked thumb toward the dangling drapery-rod.

'The drape flamed up all of a sudden,' Reddy said disgustedly. 'Everybody started jumping around and yelling for water. Some of them ran out of here. I saw it was going to catch the panel. I jerked the drape down and threw it out the window. It's outside there now.'

'And then you heard the shot and the lights went off,' Storm supplied bleakly. 'Who was in this room at the time the shot was fired? Who do you *know* was in this room?'

'Well, she was in here.' He nodded toward Karen. 'Darby was in here. Elsie and myself. Maybe Shore was,' he added slowly. 'They were *all* in here when it flamed up,' he said pointedly. 'Then they broke like cattle.'

'Who was near that window?'

'Everybody was milling around. Gordon was hunting out a deck of cards to start a game to pass the time. The rest of them were mixing around. I . . . Say, Goode! You were sitting there by that window!'

Goode's throat trembled as he swallowed. 'Yes, sir. I was,' he agreed haltingly.

'You didn't set that curtain on fire? You didn't see anyone else set it on fire?' Storm demanded.

'No, I did not, sir.'

'Go find the gun, Reddy,' Storm snapped angrily. 'Sit down, all of you.' He looked at Linda and pointed toward a chair apart from the others. As she sat down, Walt approached.

'Go back over there,' Storm said bluntly. Walt stopped and his brows snapped upward.

'Are you telling me I can't go near my wife?' he demanded.

'That's precisely what I'm doing.'

'I . . . Why, I'm damned if even a detective can — '

'Walt, please!' Linda broke in hurriedly. 'Please . . . '

He looked at her a moment, then glanced angrily at Storm. Slowly, he withdrew. Storm remained standing, staring at each person as his hard eyes moved around the semicircle of chairs.

'Now,' he began flatly. 'Where were you when that shot was fired?' He pointed at Goode.

'I was drawing a pan of water in the kitchen, sir. I had run back there when the fire blazed. I intended to bring the water up here. But that's where I was, sir,' he assured steadily.

'Gordon? Where were you?'

'I'd gotten a kettle of water. I was coming through the dining room with it when the lights went out. I stumbled and fell.' He blinked icily at Storm.

'Gabriel? Where were you?'

'I think I must have been going to the phone to call the fire department. I . . . It was all so confusing right then. I started into the hall, then I ran against someone, I believe. Yes, I remember now! I ran against someone and fell.'

'Who was that person?'

'I didn't notice. Perhaps I never saw. I don't have my glasses on — and the excitement! The fire blazed to the ceiling in less than a moment!'

Storm looked at him with disgust, then turned to Shore.

'I was in the room, as Reddy told you,' the doctor said. 'The house can burn to the foundations before I make another unaccounted move.'

'You, Karen, and Darby were in this room?'

They nodded. At that moment, the door opened and Reddy entered. 'Here it is.'

Linda looked. In the man's hand lay a short heavy pistol.

'And I don't think there'll be any fingerprints,' Reddy continued wearily. 'I found this in the hall.' He held out his other hand. There was a tan leather glove. 'They were both on the floor of the hall, back toward the kitchen door.'

'Why, that's my glove!' Shore exclaimed. 'It was in the pocket of my coat this afternoon.'

Storm looked at the gun for a long moment, then stared at the semicircle of silent people.

'One of three people in this room murdered Coke Brill — murdered him before he could reveal the killer of the woman, and of Gregory Payne. Those three people are Lester Goode, Charles Gabriel, and Walter Gordon.' He paused a moment.

'The murderer knew, when he left the study earlier, that Brill could and would reveal him. While in this room, then, he managed to set the drape on fire, creating turmoil. In the confusion, he left the room and entered the downstairs bathroom by way of the door from the hall. He closed that door, then edged open the door that led from the bathroom into the study — my back was toward that door, as was Linda Gordon's. The killer fired from that doorway, killing Brill almost instantly. The killer then shorted-out the lights in the house by jamming the metal blade of a screwdriver up into the socket of the light at the bathroom mirror. It was very simple . . . a child can short an electrical connection. The killer removed the bulb before he opened the study door; he placed the screwdriver in position. The instant he fired the shot, he needed only to move the blade an inch, and all the lights went out. Then he ran from the bath, into the dark hall, and mixed himself into the confusion that prevailed elsewhere in the house. The entire arrangement required only the simplest of planning, and swift motion — and the killer had time to plan; he knew when he left the study that he had to murder Brill before Brill talked too long.' Storm paused and pointed to the gun. 'I assume,' he said sarcastically, 'that no one claims it.'

There was no answer. Gabriel sneezed explosively.

'Has anyone here ever seen that gun before?' Storm asked.

Still there was no answer. Storm sighed. 'I didn't think so.' He gestured to Reddy. 'Clear everyone out of here except Goode, Gabriel, and Gordon. I am not saying,' he added to the others, 'that you are free of suspicion, by any means. But you will go with Reddy to Goode's quarters above the garage; stay there until you are called for. And you,' he said to Elsie Warner, 'take Mrs. Gordon upstairs and stay with her until I call you.' He glanced at Linda. 'Go upstairs. Get some sleep. Do you have any sedatives?'

'Father kept some amytal in the bathroom, but I assure you — '

'Take one and go to sleep,' he said. Linda realized it was useless to argue with him. She followed Elsie from the room and up the stairs to her bedroom. Elsie closed the door.

Linda stared at the bed, still rumpled and disturbed as it was when once before she had tried to sleep. Her eyes lifted to the window. She saw the fringe of dawn blurring the horizon. Somewhere a bird chirped faintly.

'Take it,' Elsie said firmly. Linda turned. In the girl's hand was the small amytal tablet and a glass of water. 'He meant it — you must sleep. Start undressing.' She locked the door. 'I don't mean to push you around,' she apologized with a wry smile. 'I just drop hints the blunt way. Probably an occupational habit.'

'It's all right. I just know I can't sleep, but I'll lie down if it pleases you.' Linda swallowed the tablet, pulled off her shoes, and stretched out on the bed.

Elsie crossed the room and turned off the light. The room was filled with a faint half-light from approaching dawn, and the shadow of Elsie became indistinct in the chair.

Linda felt her eyes drifting shut. 'You know . . . it was my honeymoon,' she whispered. 'But even that . . . it's not real anymore . . . '

'Sure . . . '

That was the last Linda heard.

14

Out of the restless shadow-play of dreaming, the figure of her father assumed a mystic reality in Linda's mind.

He sat at his desk, his legs crossed. He had laid aside his pen and lit a cigarette. He was smiling at her, his gray eyes twinkling. His lips moved; he was speaking, though Linda heard no words. Yet, even in sleep, she felt herself responding, smiling back at him, answering. And she felt a queer, shy wave of pathos fill her throat. For she knew, strangely, that soon he was to die.

And then Linda felt her breath drain slowly from her throat. She felt her hands grip the arms of her chair. With hypnotic fixity her eyes turned toward the hall door. The door was opening . . .

A figure was entering. Linda could not see his face; there, in the dream, her eyes blurred. She could see his hand, the shining knife in his fingers. She watched him moving, gliding without a sound toward her father. She tried to scream. No sound came from her lips, and still her father smiled at her, oblivious of the stranger coming from behind. Linda felt cold perspiration streaming from her face. And still she saw the knife, rising! Starting down! Plunging toward her father's back! With a frenzied horror that seemed to rip itself from the depths of her stomach, she screamed at last!

'Father! He's killing you! Move! *Move* — '

'Now, now! Stop! Wake up! It's all right now!'

Her eyes opened wide. Like a harsh physical blow, the glaring sunlight poured into her vision. Above her was the half-remembered face of Elsie Warner; the girl was speaking to her, shaking her shoulder. Linda trembled.

'A man! He was killing my father! He — '

'No, you were just dreaming. It's all over now,' Elsie assured firmly.

Slowly, a cold, flat reality began to sink into Linda's mind. Her fingers crept up to her cheeks. They were hot and damp. The sun flooded the room, and the air was sticky and listless. 'What time is it?' she whispered.

'Oh, it's after three in the afternoon. You had a long nap.'

'After three!' Linda struggled to sit up. 'Has anything happened whilst I slept?'

'Nothing at all,' Elsie assured. 'Storm is in New York; don't ask me why. The others, except Goode, are out in Goode's quarters with Reddy. I suppose they've been sleeping too.'

'Oh . . . I'll get up. Take a bath and dress,' Linda decided mechanically. She started across the room, then stopped as she passed the mirror. A hard shock went through her as she looked at her own image.

Her golden-brown eyes were dull and lusterless, deeply shadowed. Her hair was limp and loose. The clothes in which she had slept were wrinkled. *I look old*, she thought silently.

She pulled her eyes from the mirror and took fresh underwear from the dresser. She found a light cotton dress in the closet, then entered the bathroom.

247

Slowly, she undressed and turned on the shower. She stepped under the needles of cold water. Her breath caught. She could almost feel the dark fragments of nightmare slide away, and she breathed more deeply now. At last she turned off the water.

She dressed slowly and brushed her hair. Finally, she opened the door and stepped back into the bedroom. Elsie glanced up.

'I was just getting ready to call you. Storm is back. He asked me to bring you downstairs.'

'I'm ready,' Linda said. They left the room. They moved through the silent house and to the sunporch.

Storm rose from a chair, 'Good morning. Or afternoon,' he corrected wearily.

'Hello.' Linda looked at him steadily as he sat down again. A dark shadow of beard coated his jaws and chin. His hair was disordered. His collar was open, his tie pulled down to one side, his clothes dusty and wrinkled. His eyes were haggard and sleepless, and a stained cigarette hung in his fingers.

Elsie departed. Linda sat down and waited. For a moment she thought Storm was sinking into sleep. Then he pulled himself erect and shook his head roughly.

'You'd better eat. Or have you?' he asked.

'No. I just got up.' She turned. 'Goode?' she called toward the kitchen. The man appeared, dark-eyed and ashen-faced.

'Yes, Miss Linda?'

'I just want some juice and coffee, please.'

'Yes, Miss Linda.' He withdrew. Storm mashed out his cigarette and lit another.

'You're twenty-three, aren't you?' he said. Linda nodded. 'How long have you known Walter Gordon?'

Linda's eyes widened in surprise. 'Nearly two years.'

'Tell me what you know of his background.'

'Well, his parents are dead. They died about three years ago, I think. His father was a small rancher in Texas — their place was somewhere near Amarillo.'

'Music his only work?'

'Yes. When he was young, he decided he wanted to be a musician. His mother approved and he took lessons in Texas until he was twenty. Then he said he wanted to come to New York to study. His father disapproved; he wanted Walt to remain there and help him with the ranch. It was the cause of some bitterness, I understand. But, anyway, Walt came. After two years, he managed to get a scholarship at the Garallino Academy in New York. When that was over, he gave a few small concerts. He had little money, so he often taught a few pupils to help out financially. All of this time he was composing — his main ambition is to write music. Then . . . it was three years ago . . . Walt's mother and father both died. He was the only child, and the ranch was his. He sold it. In the end, I think he got around thirty thousand dollars. For the first time he had enough money to do as he wished. He took a trip to South and Central America, studying the native music of the countries, going far into the interior to search for tribal music. A little less than two years ago, he returned. He was lecturing on his trip at the Warburn Guild when I met him. We saw each other more and more. We ... got married;' she finished simply.

'Was there any discussion of financial affairs before you and Walter Gordon were married?' Storm wondered.

'Yes. He told me how much money he had; it is about twenty-five thousand dollars now. From that, he gets around a thousand dollars a year income in dividends. He explained that he could easily make another two or three thousand a year by taking pupils in the mornings, leaving the afternoons free for composing. He said that would total around four thousand dollars, and he considered it enough.'

'What did you think? Or your father?' Storm asked.

Linda smiled faintly. 'I didn't care a great deal what Walt made, but father talked to me about it after Walt had explained to him. Father said Walt had no idea what it would cost to support me, to buy or keep a house, to pay taxes

— anything like that. Father went on to explain that musicians were not likely to be great financial successes. Father wasn't being critical about it,' she explained swiftly. 'He was just advising me. He told me I would have to use a lot of tact and discretion after I was married, because my money and income would have to be used to supplement Walt's. He approved of the marriage. He was just giving me some practical suggestions.' She hesitated and watched Storm's tired face. 'Why are you asking me about Walt?' she asked slowly. 'Has anything happened to make you think — '

'Oh, no. Nothing you haven't heard already,' he said bleakly. 'I suppose I'm seeing skeletons everywhere. But the fact remains,' he added doggedly, 'that your husband was one of the three men who could have murdered Coke Brill. I keep running up against that fact.' He tapped the table nervously and scowled. 'Damn it, I might have traded with Brill, but . . . But how could I trust him, with all his — '

'Storm! Come here, Storm!' Reddy's

furious shouts erupted from the window of Goode's apartment above the garage. Storm jerked from his chair, sending it crashing back to the floor. He leaped across the sunporch and out of the door. Linda rose quickly. She followed him across the gravel driveway, into the doorway, and up the narrow flight of stairs.

' . . . found him there on the floor! Don't know when he got there or how!' Reddy was saying angrily. A door slammed in the apartment. Linda hurried into Goode's small, neat living room.

They were standing against the far wall — Karen and Darby and Charles Gabriel and Clifton Shore. A solitaire layout was scrambled on the table. A chair lay on the floor. Darby's face was white. Karen was rigid. Gabriel's cheeks were flushed, and his chest heaved to his hard breathing. Shore was utterly motionless. All of them were tired-faced, the men unshaven, their collars open, the faces perspiring.

And, in another doorway leading deeper into the apartment, stood a flushed and panting Reddy.

'I happened to count noses and saw he was gone,' he was saying. 'I prowled around, and there he was.'

A cold, chilling fear shot through Linda as her mind grasped the fact. They were talking about Walt!

She stumbled across the room. 'Where is — Oh, God, no!' she screamed as she saw him. He lay on the tile floor of the bathroom, his legs and arms half beneath him, his face down. And across the glistening floor stretched the thin, dark rivulet that was blood.

'Oh, God, he's not — ' she cried.

'No, no! It's all right. He's just unconscious,' Storm interrupted sharply. He was kneeling down, turning Walt's head. Linda saw the short gash in the temple, the stain of blood on the cheek and chin. She swayed and gripped the door. Then she was beside him, speaking to him, asking him to wake.

Storm's firm hands pulled her erect. 'Please! Don't get hysterical. It's just a slight injury. He'll be all right in a few minutes. He — ' His harassed eyes roamed to Reddy, then beyond him to the silent people in the living room. 'You don't know who was in here when it happened?' he snapped angrily.

Reddy flushed and shook his head. 'I'm sorry as hell. I didn't notice a thing until — '

'Well, find out what you can,' Storm interrupted. 'Shore,' he called, 'come here and help me. Take a look.'

'We've got to take him to the house,' Linda said firmly. 'Either that or I come out here.'

'We'll take him to the house,' Storm assured her.

He held her away as Shore entered the small bathroom and knelt down beside Walt. Linda watched his fingers gently probing about the wound. Presently the doctor looked up.

'Nothing serious,' he said. 'He'll come around in a few minutes. It's perfectly safe to move him now, if you wish.'

'You can help me carry him. I . . . ' Storm paused and peered into the wastebasket. 'Who's been burning paper in here?' he demanded.

There was no answer. Storm cursed

under his breath. 'Reddy, find out what he was slugged with. It's in this apartment, or was thrown from a window. But *do not* leave the apartment. If you can't find it inside, call me. And keep them together if you have to break their legs,' he snapped. He gestured to Dr. Shore.

They bent over Walt's still figure, took a firm grip, and lifted him. Linda followed through the living room, down the stairs, and across the drive to the sunporch.

As they entered, Goode hurried out of the kitchen. His hands fluttered nervously.

'Go back to the kitchen where you were,' Storm said impatiently. They pushed past Goode and turned up the stairs in the hall. Linda hurried ahead and opened the door of the bedroom. Swiftly, she folded back the covers. They let the still figure down gently.

'I'll take you back to Goode's quarters,' Storm said to Shore. They departed. Linda got a damp towel from the bath. Walt moaned.

Storm returned soon and leaned

against the wall. He smoked, and his eyes were dark with silent fury as they watched Walt.

'If he's not hurt seriously, why doesn't he wake up?' Linda asked breathlessly. 'It's been ten minutes at least! We don't know how long it was before — '

Walt groaned heavily. His fingers trembled and clutched at emptiness. His lips parted and twitched as though he were trying to speak. His arms jerked. Abruptly, his mouth opened and he gasped: 'Don't! Don't do that!' His eyes fluttered open, and Linda looked down into their startled depths.

'It's all right. It's me, Walt,' she whispered. 'It's all right now.'

His glance jerked around the walls, the ceiling. Slowly, the hardness in his face faded.

'You,' he said vacantly. 'But where . . . Who . . . In that bathroom . . . the smoke in the wastebasket and . . . '

Storm stepped forward. 'What happened, Gordon?'

Walt stared at him dully. 'I don't know what happened . . . I was dozing in a chair. Some of them were playing cards, and the radio was going. I got up to go to the bathroom. I turned the knob. The door acted as if it was locked. I guess I gave it a hard push. It seemed to hang a second, then opened, as if it had been just half-bolted. I walked in and closed it behind me. When I turned, I saw the smoke fuming up out of the wastebasket. I bent over and saw scraps of paper shriveling into ashes. Then . . . just while I was bending over there, I heard a sound. I started to turn . . . saw the curtain of the shower moving. Then something hit me. I never got to look up and see who . . . what it was.' Walt blinked dully and touched his temple. 'I can't remember anything else. My head . . . aches,' he whispered heavily.

'Can you remember who was in the living room when you left to go to the bath?' Storm asked.

'Reddy was there. Karen was playing cards, I think. Maybe Darby was with her, or watching her. Then the others . . . ' He stopped and frowned. 'I'm not sure where the others were. The radio was going. I can't remember.'

'You couldn't tell what the burning paper had been?'

'It had writing on it. I saw traces of words, written in ink — but didn't get to read them. They were disappearing as the fire ate the paper up.'

Storm shrugged impatiently and turned away. Walt's eyes closed and his fingers relaxed on the sheet. Linda glanced at Storm. He gestured silently toward the hall door. Reluctantly she rose and started across the room. Storm lowered the shades at the windows, throwing the room into dim half-shadows.

'Where . . . you're leaving, Linda?' Walt asked.

'We'll be in the next room if you want us,' Storm said.

'Could I have some aspirin? My head keeps aching.'

Linda turned toward the bathroom. She brought him water and the small white tablets. At last, she followed Storm from the room, and the detective closed the door. Together they entered the next room — the room that had been Mr.

Payne's bedroom.

Storm lit another cigarette and rubbed his stubbled chin distractedly. 'We were talking about the three men who could have murdered Coke Brill,' he reminded her wearily. 'What about Goode? How long has he been here?'

'Goode? Oh, for years — since before I was born,' Linda said quickly. 'It simply couldn't be Goode. Father trusted him implicitly. He's the most gentle creature in the world. It couldn't be Goode.'

Storm looked at her with a faint hint of irony. 'So you leave me with no one but Gabriel. A successful lawyer, senior partner of his firm; wealthy, respectable, if reactionary . . . He won't fit into the murder role so well.'

'The truth is,' Linda said slowly, 'no one fits very well. Have you considered that it might be someone outside?'

'Off and on, of course,' Storm admitted restlessly. 'But I keep remembering the dead woman's warning to your father. She was emphatic that he tell none of his friends of her visit, even though he called the police. Then she was killed. Brill didn't kill her. And when he was ready to reveal who did, he was killed himself.' Storm gestured roughly. 'No! It's got to be one of the people in this housed!' He paced the room, frowning.

'I went to that filling station where Brill found the evidence,' he said. 'The filling station was rented last Friday. The new tenant has cleaned up the place. He says there were half a dozen old oil drums. He sold them all to a scrap-metal company in New York. They've been removed. It would be almost impossible to find that certain drum, to find any fingerprints still intact. Furthermore, the new man's painted the place, ruining any prints that might have been on the window that the killer crawled through, if Brill was telling the truth.'

'What about the evidence? Brill said he had it. If you — '

'That's what I was doing in New York all morning,' Storm interrupted bleakly. 'I searched that uptown apartment where we caught him. I searched his rooms at the Golden Owl. I even got into his club — the Sparrow Inn on East Thirty-Third.

261

I found nothing. With his criminal cunning, Brill would have gone to unimaginable trouble to cache his proof. If I only had some idea . . .

'It was proof that couldn't be framed by anybody, Brill said. Now, what kind of proof is that?' Storm looked at Linda steadily. 'Something he fished out of the drum? Something he found because the material in the drum pointed to it? And whatever it was, how could it be so unique that its information was immediately undeniable and incorruptible?'

'I'm sure I don't know,' Linda admitted. 'You didn't find any fingerprints on the gun that your assistant turned up after Brill's death?'

'None at all, nor any suggestion as to whose gun it was. The killer has been so damned careful! If he would make one slip! If he — '

The ringing of the telephone in the hall broke his words. He turned and hurried from the room. Linda heard him talking:

'Yes . . . Storm speaking . . . On the woman . . . ? You're sure? And how about number one . . . ? Damn . . . And number two . . . ?' There was a weary sigh. 'No, thanks. That's all . . . Goodbye.' The receiver clicked. Storm's footsteps came slowly along the hall. He entered the room and closed the door.

'That was Headquarters in New York. I took them some fingerprints this morning. They report that they can't find anything against the woman's prints that I took from her suitcase. They have no record of your husband's fingerprints, nor of Goode's,' he finished.

'You had Walt's fingerprints checked by the police?' Linda exclaimed strangely.

Storm nodded. 'I told you I was seeing skeletons.'

Linda closed her eyes. It was like a shadow of poison, this figure of suspicion that cast itself first here, then there, and spared no one. And it seemed to Linda that some fragment of the shadow remained on everyone, like a scar across the faces of those she long had loved. And she thought of Walt.

Her fingers clenched themselves against her palms.

Then Storm's voice was filling the hot

room again: 'According to Darby, it was after ten o'clock that Saturday night of May the sixth when he awakened to find himself at the well-grave with Brill. That would suggest that Brill saw the killer sometime between nine and ten. I've questioned all of them regarding that period. The answers . . . ' He paused and pulled a limp notebook from his pocket.

'Shore went to a show that night. He can't remember what he saw — some war picture, he thinks. He went alone. His story can't be confirmed . . . Goode, as you remember, had been sent from this house in anticipation of the woman's visit on one of those nights. He, too, attended a show — the one in Warburn. He remembers it very well, but the same show was the previous night, when Goode was again away from the house. He could have seen it then. He says he simply walked that first night. And as to Gabriel,' Storm continued, 'he tells me he was at home in New York with his wife. He spent that evening studying a legal brief. We know where Darby was. And your husband says he was ill in his New

York apartment.' Storm cocked a brow. 'What do you know about that?'

'Ill?' Linda echoed. 'I don't . . . Oh! That was the day after he'd been out here for dinner. I remember now. He came to dinner Friday evening. He didn't eat. After dinner he asked for some aspirin. Later, he asked if we had a thermometer. I gave him Father's and he took his temperature. It was a hundred-point-something. He went home early. I called him the next afternoon, and he was in bed. It was a slight throat infection, he said.'

'Did you see the thermometer?'

'I certainly did,' Linda assured him steadily. 'It's hard to read — hard to find the mercury. I read it for him. I felt his face and hands. They were hot and moist and clammy.'

Storm regarded her intently for a full ten seconds, then finally he smiled apologetically. 'I assure you I'm not trying to make a goat of your husband, Mrs. Gordon. I've got to know these things . . . ' He paused and looked at his watch. 'Ten until five,' he murmured slowly. He looked out of the window. 'Not much longer . . . '

'Not much longer until what?' Linda asked.

'Until I must let the police know about Brill. I've made myself a deadline of nine tonight. At that, there's going to be the unmitigated devil to pay. And the hell of it is,' Storm growled, 'I know they won't get anywhere either. Maybe I'm an egotistical jackass, but if I can't . . . ' He stopped and sighed wearily. 'One man here is making a jackass of me,' he admitted sourly.

Linda felt a strange wave of compassion for this tired and angry man. She wondered how long it had been since he had eaten, rested, slept. 'I wish there was something I could do to help,' she said sincerely.

'Thanks.' He mashed out his cigarette. 'I'm going to make one last try at that brassiere-and-slip thing. That's all I've got left.' He crossed the room and opened the hall door. 'Elsie!' he shouted. A door opened downstairs.

'Yes?' the girl called.

'Go out to the garage. See what Reddy's learned on the slugging. And bring Dr. Shore back her with you. Bring him up here.'

'Right,' the girl called. Storm leaned against the wall and closed his eyes. Linda watched him in silence, and the shadows grew long across the floor as the sun dropped deeper in the west.

'I'm sorry about this — what it's doing to you,' Storm said quietly. Linda glanced up, surprised at the grave depth of Storm's tone. Then his fingers touched her shoulder gently. 'It shouldn't have happened to anyone like you.'

Linda started to speak. Then she realized there was nothing to say.

15

'You'd better look in on Gordon,' Storm suggested when Dr. Shore appeared. 'You wait with Mrs. Gordon, Elsie.'

The girl came into the bedroom. She and Linda nodded. They did not speak. Linda listened to the movements in the next room. Presently, Storm and Shore returned. The detective nodded to Shore to sit down, then looked at Elsie. Linda watched Storm's face.

'What had Reddy found?'

'Mr. Gordon was hit with a small wrench. Reddy didn't find it; I found it, in the weeds about twenty feet away from the bathroom window. Reddy says there won't be any prints. A washrag was twisted around the handle; it was still there when I found it. And Goode says he took the wrench to the bathroom to fix a connection yesterday; he forgot to put it back in the garage.'

'Reddy found out nothing about the burned paper?'

Elsie shook her head. 'Nor about who was in the bathroom.'

'About par,' Storm snapped icily. 'That's all. Close the door.' The girl left the room quickly. Storm turned toward the haggard, unshaven Shore. 'It's after five,' he said tonelessly. 'At nine tonight, I'm calling in the police. I've got four hours of my own . . . I think you realize how dangerous will be your position when the police enter this case. They will be asked to pass judgment on your tale of faking the suicide scene in this room the afternoon Payne was killed. They will be told of your disposal of your gun. If you have found me blunt, you will find them infinitely more so. You know all that?'

'I know,' Shore said. His voice was low and thick.

'I'm going to ask you to think, to try to help me. If you are innocent, you realize how important it is for you to give all the help you can.'

'I do. I will.'

'I have one maze of facts, one tangle of inexplicable conduct. It's possible that you, as a doctor, may see a meaning in it that is not apparent to me.' Storm moved his chair nearer to Shore.

'Before Payne was murdered, a woman came to this house to warn him of a danger which threatened Linda and himself. She did not reveal that danger; she was attempting blackmail, and Payne ordered her away. He reconsidered and decided to see her. When she tried to return, she was murdered. Her body was hidden in an abandoned well on Glenn Darby's property. Then evidence of violence was discovered by Goode, and Payne called me into the case. I was able to locate the hotel room where the unknown woman had lived for a short time — the Sequin Arms in Greenwich Village. By the time I found her room, all her possessions had been removed. All the furniture, floor, the window, even the bathroom had been carefully cleaned. No clue remained to identify her.

'Yesterday at noon, I found her body in the well-grave. She had been brutally clubbed to death about the head and face. She could not be identified, so disfiguring were the injuries to her face.

But here are other facts I did learn from the body. The woman's dress buttoned at the front. When I discovered the body, the buttons were improperly fastened, one having been skipped. Upon further examination, I learned that there was no undergarment on the upper part of the woman's body — no slip or brassiere. Since the dress buttoned at the front and the buttons were fairly widely spaced, it seemed at least a questionable way for a woman to be dressed. And then I discovered the most curious and inexplicable fact of all. On the left side of the body, on the flesh that covered the ribs, I found a network, a latticework, of light cuts or scratches. There were perhaps thirty of these cuts. To picture them, imagine a woven rectangle of coarse wool about four inches by five in size.' Storm paused and leaned forward, lifting one finger.

'No bandage protected this network of cuts, yet the inner side of the woman's dress was scarcely soiled at all. Secondly, though there was no bandage, I could see traces of a pinkish tint on the flesh which had, in tiny places, escaped the knife. It appeared that some antiseptic, some medication had been applied to the flesh. Now ... why, if the cuts had been treated, was there no bandage on the injury? And why, since there was no bandage, had the inner side of the dress escaped almost all stains?'

The doctor swallowed. 'Is that all?' he asked slowly.

'No.' Storm lit another cigarette. 'We now go back to the night the woman was murdered. Coke Brill was visiting Glenn Darby that evening. As matters developed, Brill happened to see a man creep to the window of Darby's house and peer in. Apparently the man satisfied himself that Darby was drunk and unconscious; further, the stranger did not observe Brill. The man withdrew. For reasons of his own, Brill trailed the man. The man went to the well-grave. As he cautiously used a flashlight, Brill saw him wielding a knife, and removing some garments from the body.' Storm paused and raised his finger again. 'From that we can assume that the man Brill was watching — the murderer

— was at that time inflicting the network of scratches on the left side of the body. We can also assume that he was removing the slip and brassiere . . . Finally, the man covered the body with soil and rocks. He departed, and Brill trailed him. The man was carrying a bundle. At a vacant filling station on the lane that passes Darby's house, the man disposed of the bundle and continued on. As Brill passed the filling station, he noticed the glow of a fire in the depths of the building; he likewise noticed that the man carried no bundle now. Quickly, Brill entered the building. From an oil drum he salvaged the burning material. There were some clothes, men's clothes, wet and bloody. There was a woman's cloth purse. There was a brassiere and the remains of a slip.'

'So the man had taken the slip and brassiere!' Shore said.

'He had. And from the material that Brill salvaged, he was able to identify the dead woman. Furthermore, he was able to establish a connection between the dead woman and the man who had killed her. That connection is unknown to me.

273

It is of absolute and vital importance to my solution of this case,' Storm said with flat finality. 'Before Brill was shot, he dropped one faint clue — a clue which may or may not have a bearing. He said he had learned what was the matter with the woman . . . I attempted to press him. He shied away, indicating that the point was of importance. He was stalling for a bargain with me before he made revelations.

'Now I come to the one final piece of the pattern — if it is a pattern,' Storm qualified gloomily. 'I had discovered the room in Greenwich Village where the woman had lived for a few days, remember?' Shore nodded quickly. He was watching Storm intently. 'I told you that all possessions of the woman had been removed. Well . . . after I discovered the body yesterday and noticed that there was no brassiere and slip, I experimented with the longshot chance that those garments had been removed to prevent an identification of the woman. I reasoned that perhaps the woman's other brassieres and slips might bear some curious or peculiar clues of identification. If so, the killer would have removed them from her room. But if he had removed only slips and brassieres, he would have called attention to the absence of those garments. To avoid such attention, perhaps the killer decided to clean the room completely, take everything in order to shield the theft of exactly what was necessary to take.

'After considering that possibility, I asked myself the question: Is it not difficult in New York City to destroy a suitcase, shoes, heavy clothes? Not impossible, certainly. Wouldn't one think it safer to park them, more or less permanently, out of sight? But to destroy light garments such as slips and brassieres presented no problem at all — burn them in a wastebasket; shred them and flush them down a toilet. So finally I reasoned that the killer might have destroyed only the slips and brassieres, and elsewhere we might find the suitcase. My reasoning, for once in this case, was accurate. The woman's suitcase was found. And it contained *no* slips and *no* brassieres. So the thread of consistency still holds: These certain items had been removed, from the woman and from her stock of clothes. There must have been a reason for this, and also for the mutilation of the woman's left side. But is there a connection between those two facts? If so, what is the connection?' Storm paused.

'That is the problem you are putting to me?' Shore asked.

Storm nodded. 'It's hard to say what I'm driving at — I'm only feeling along in the dark. But Brill said there was something the matter with the woman. Could it have been anything relating to the slips and brassieres? Or could it have had some connection with the mutilation which the killer felt it was necessary to inflict?'

Shore leaned back with a puzzled frown. 'I don't know. The parts seem so incongruous. I . . . ' He blinked suddenly. 'A tattoo! Had you thought of that? That pink tint you noticed, could it — '

Storm interrupted Shore with a weary shake of his head. 'I thought of that at the time. I inspected the pinkish flesh carefully. It wasn't a tattoo.'

'You don't think the killer was a sex criminal of some kind, who merely removed the woman's clothes and mutilated . . . No, no, of course not,' Shore agreed as Storm shook his head again.

Once more, Shore leaned back. 'You know something was wrong with the woman. You know that her slips and brassieres have been taken. Her left side was mutilated,' he mused aloud.

'And I'm asking if you know of any illness or injury which would have left some evidence or proof on the woman's undergarments. Proof which would have led to an identification of some accomplice, some associate, some man related to her.'

'Let us assume,' Shore said suddenly, 'that her identifying injury, as we shall call it, was located on that mutilated left side. Now. What facts are essential if our assumption is to fulfill the facts you know of? First, the injury had to mark all the slips and brassieres, else why were all of them stolen? Women usually have how many slips and brassieres? Say five or six of each. Assume that this woman changed each day. It would have taken at least five or six days to mark all slips and brassieres. Furthermore, the injury had to be active all that time. If it was some peculiar sore, it had to bleed or run every day. Therefore, we conclude that the injury was of a semi-constant nature.' He paused and tapped the chair arms.

'Second, the injury must have been unique, rare, and serious. A normal blemish or sore might have been treated by the woman herself, and would have been unknown to anyone else. The injury was treated; we must conclude that. It was treated by a specialist, shall we say. Of course! Don't you see?' he exclaimed. 'It was an injury which called for treatment by a specialist. The killer knew it would be recognized as such. He knew that an observer, seeing the injury, would be able to know where to go for full information concerning the woman . . . Not simply to a doctor, but to a certain kind of doctor. And the killer knew that such a doctor must not be questioned! Do you follow me? The secret is with the specialist who was treating the woman. Find that man, Storm, and I predict he will have information that will lead you to recognize the killer.'

'So we want a specialist,' Storm murmured acidly. 'But what kind? You've gotten somewhere, but not far enough.'

'Yes, of course . . . Did Payne ever see this woman?'

'Once.'

'Was there anything peculiar about her? Any deformity?'

'No. She was plain and undistinctive. Payne recalled that she used lilac-scented perfume. She was rigid in posture. Her diction was good. She . . . Oh, yes. She had a cold the night she visited him. And the manager of the Sequin remarked that he'd heard her coughing. When I found her body, there were a few tissues folded in her pocket. But you can't identify a woman on the basis of a cold.'

'No.' Shore shifted uneasily in his chair. 'I'll try to think,' he said slowly.

'Time is not unlimited,' Storm reminded him wearily. He looked at his watch, then his eyes moved to the window. Linda straightened in her chair. She realized suddenly that the room was dim; the sun was gone from the sky. Now the darkness brought a tired and hopeless fear that was edged with anxiety for the few hours left until nine. She realized then, for the first time, that she felt a firm and silent faith in this man, John Storm. She dreaded the heavy footsteps that would bring the police.

Storm stood up. 'We'll leave you to think, Shore,' he said. Linda rose. Together they left the room, and Shore was alone in the gathering darkness.

In the hall, Storm sighed. 'I suppose Goode might as well fix something to eat,' he said listlessly.

'Let me see if Walt's all right, then I'll go down and help.' Linda opened the door and peered into the shadows toward the bed. 'Are you awake, Walt?' she asked softly.

The bed creaked. 'Um. Linda?' he murmured.

She crossed the room and snapped on the bed-lamp. He blinked and shielded his eyes. The cut on his head was bandaged now. He was undressed. A sheet half-covered him.

'Was sleeping,' he said drowsily. 'Anything the matter?'

'I just wanted to see how you were, darling.' She bent over him. 'Goode's going to fix something. Are you hungry?'

'I don't . . . No,' he decided. 'My head keeps aching. You'll come back, won't you?'

'In just a few minutes,' she promised. She kissed him. She turned out the light and tiptoed back across the room to the door. In the shadows she stumbled into Storm.

'Oh, I didn't see,' she gasped. 'I'm sorry, I — '

'That lamp . . . Your hand made no shadow on the wall,' he whispered in a voice that was stark, raw with incredulity. She could not see his features. Only the rigid stillness of him as he stood there told her how tense he was, and the rawness of his whispers swept her breath away.

'No shadow on the wall . . . And your father saw the shadow! The shadow of the hand plunging the knife toward his back! But he couldn't . . . *couldn't*! You understand that! *Your father was lying!*' Storm said viciously. 'Oh, God! I've been a blind idiot!'

'What do you mean? My father wouldn't lie — ' Linda began.

'Come in here!' Storm seized her arm. He almost jerked her from her feet as he spun back toward Gregory Payne's bedroom and threw open the door.

'What is — ?' Shore began.

'Go somewhere else to do your thinking. Downstairs.' Storm snapped on the overhead light and gestured impatiently. The doctor departed. Storm turned to Linda, his brown eyes alight with intense speculation.

'Don't you see? I saw it when you turned on the lamp by Walt's bed. The lamp was between you and the wall. Thus, you threw no shadow on the wall. And the lamp on your father's desk! It was between him and the wall. And the killer — the attempted killer — was even further behind your father. So there could *not* have been a shadow of the arm and knife! Remember, your father said he threw the lamp and plunged the room into darkness! Thus the overhead light had been off all the time. Only the lamp had been burning. It couldn't have thrown the shadow! So your father's story of the attempted murder becomes a lie. What a thick-headed ass I've been!'

16

'But my father never lied!' Linda exclaimed. 'He simply never told — '

Storm's gesture interrupted her protest. 'Is there another lamp in the house like the one that was on your father's desk?'

'I think so . . . in the bedroom across the hall,' Linda recalled.

'Stay here.' Storm strode from the room. Half a minute later he returned with a lamp. It was table-size, about thirty inches tall, with a round metal base, an inverted white-glass reflector, and a tan shade. 'Now, show me where your father's lamp stayed.'

Linda crossed the room to the flat-topped writing desk. She pointed to a place on the left side of the desk, about midway between the back and front. Storm set the lamp at that place and plugged it into the wall-socket.

'Now, look,' he said swiftly. 'This desk

is in the corner; anyone who sits here is facing the wall. His back is toward the room, and toward the door from the hall. And see . . . the lamp is between him and the wall. Now . . . ' Storm snapped on the lamp, then crossed the room to turn out the overhead light. 'Sit down at that desk. Take out a sheet of paper. Your father said he had been writing a letter. Place your arm there . . . right! Now, watch the wall ahead of you — that's where he said he saw the shadow.'

From his pocket he drew a knife and opened the blade. Slowly he approached Linda's back, lifting his right hand and arm. His eyes were fixed on the brightly lighted wall beyond the desk. He stopped when he was less than a foot from Linda's chair. His arm came slowly down with the knife — down until the point of the blade touched her shoulders.

'See! No shadow!' he breathed. 'The man could have killed your father without making a shadow. Look . . . ' He raised the knife again. He reached forward, across Linda's shoulder. The knife passed her face, and still there was no shadow.

Not until Storm had reached halfway across the desk, beyond the lamp, did the shadow of his hand appear on the wall.

'I see!' Linda realized breathlessly. She turned to face Storm. 'But . . . but then . . . Why did he tell you that?' she stammered.

'Yes. *Why?*' Storm murmured slowly. 'I remember his story perfectly. He'd been writing, he said. It was nine-thirty. He was sitting at this desk, this table. Suddenly he saw the shadow of an arm racing down the wall, plunging toward his back. He twisted and turned, just in time to avoid the lunge of a knife. There was a masked man behind him. He grasped the lamp and hurled it at the man. The room was plunged into darkness. Your father tried to get the gun he kept in the drawer here. The man escaped . . . That was your father's story.' Storm paused. His eyes gleamed at the lamp, at the table, at the wall. Linda scarcely breathed.

'So why did he lie to me about a matter of such deadly importance? Because he was striving, in his lie, to reveal to me some hidden truth . . . ? But why was it necessary for him to be so indirect? We were alone in this room; he could have spoken frankly to . . . ' His words stopped as a sudden new thought jammed his speech.

'We were *not* alone!' he exploded furiously. His eyes raked the room. Abruptly, he strode to the closet and jerked open the door. He stepped inside and drew the door half-shut. 'Yes! I can see the desk chair!' he exclaimed. 'And your father never left that chair the entire time I was here that afternoon! He — '

Suddenly Storm strode across the room and stepped into the hall. 'Goode! Goode, come up here!' he shouted. 'At once!'

Moments later the frantic patter of footsteps sounded on the stairs. A gray-faced and perspiring Goode appeared.

'You called me, sir?' he panted.

'I did. Sit down,' Storm said briskly. He shut the hall door, lit a cigarette, and perched his foot in the seat of a chair as he faced Goode intently.

'Gregory Payne was murdered on the afternoon of the thirteenth, you remember,' he began crisply. 'At a little after three that afternoon, you left this house and went into Warburn to take a train for Albany. Right?'

'Yes, sir. At about three-ten,' Goode said.

'Tell me everything Payne did that day, from the time you first saw him that morning until you left this house that afternoon. Don't leave out anything. Now . . . '

'I . . . I came in from my rooms about eight in the morning, as usual,' Goode began haltingly. 'I prepared Mr. Payne's customary breakfast. As you know, Miss Linda was away in New York. At eight-fifteen the breakfast was ready, but Mr. Payne had not come down. I came up here to call him. I knocked on this door. He told me he had gotten no sleep, that he felt ill. He asked me to bring his breakfast up. I did, sir.' Goode paused, mopped at his damp chin. 'I brought the tray in here. Mr. Payne seemed rather . . . well, ill at ease. Nervous, disinclined to talk. But he did say he had worried all night about Miss Linda.'

'Where was Payne when you were in this room?'

'Oh, he was there — standing over there beside the bed.'

'The bed.' Storm glanced in that direction, then measured its distance to the closet. He nodded slightly. 'Go on.'

'I went back downstairs and ate my own breakfast. At nine I returned to this room for Mr. Payne's tray. It was then that he told me of his plan to go into New York for a week or so. He told me I might have a vacation during that time. He asked me to drive into Warburn and get him a ticket for the seven-ten train that evening. I . . . I believe it was then that he told me I could leave that afternoon,' Goode remembered firmly. 'I offered to remain and help him pack. He declined. He said he would take very little to New York. He seemed rather blunt, as though he wished me to go as soon as possible. He said he was going to take a walk outside, to get his mind clear. He did seem so worried, sir,' Goode stressed anxiously.

'Hmm . . . going for a walk.' Storm frowned, then shrugged. 'Where was Payne when you were in this room that time?'

'At that desk, sir,' Goode remembered.

'Did he move from the desk while you were in the room?'

'I don't think so, sir. I believe not.'

'All right. Go on.'

'I took the tray downstairs, fetched my hat and coat, and used my car to drive into Warburn. I suppose I left here about nine-thirty. I was gone about an hour in all; I did a bit of shopping for myself — a new shirt, socks . . . ' He mopped at his chin again. 'At one o'clock I came up to inform Mr. Payne that his lunch was ready. He . . . He seemed most upset now, sir. His fingers were trembling. He talked most queerly — breathlessly. He said he couldn't come down. He told me to bring something up on a tray. I gave him his train ticket. He scarcely seemed to see it, or remember that he'd asked me to buy it — '

'Had he taken a walk?' Storm interrupted.

'Yes, sir. While I was in Warburn. So I — '

'How do you know he'd taken a walk?' Storm demanded.

'The front door was open when I

returned. It had been closed and locked when I left. Mr. Payne's walking stick was on the hall-table downstairs, whereas it had been in the umbrella stand. And Mr. Payne was dressed at lunch, while he had been wearing his robe and pajamas at breakfast.'

'I see,' Storm said slowly. 'And where was Payne while you were in this room at one o'clock?'

'He was sitting in that chair, sir; there at the desk. He was very stiff. He hardly moved at all, never left the chair while I was here.'

'And you say he appeared much more nervous and uneasy at noon than he had at breakfast?'

'Markedly so, sir.'

'All right. Continue.'

'He asked me when I was leaving. I told him I would go on the three-thirty train. Then he told me he was expecting you. He instructed me to bring you up to this room. That was all he said, I believe. I returned to the kitchen. At about one-forty I came back up here to remove his tray. He was still seated at the desk, sir

. . . He did not move. I can't recall that he spoke the entire time . . . but he did later,' Goode recalled.

'I removed the tray. I saw him no more until I brought you up at two o'clock. I believe you were with him until about three. Immediately after you left, I came up to inform him that my cab had come and I was leaving. I asked if there was anything I could do. He said there was nothing. He . . . And he reminded me to fill the salt shaker. That was all. I left him. He was sitting at the desk, just as he had been. And I . . . that was the last time I saw him, sir,' Goode finished softly.

'He reminded you to fill the salt shaker?' Storm echoed. He frowned slightly. 'And did you?'

'Yes, sir. Before I went to my cab, I paused in the kitchen to do that.'

Storm continued to frown. 'Was it empty?'

'Yes, sir. I suppose I'd overlooked filling it.'

Storm tapped his fingers against his knee. 'Have you forgotten anything?' he asked carefully. 'What about a broken lamp? Didn't you — '

'Oh, yes, sir! That was stupid of me!' Goode apologized. 'When I came up with the lunch tray, I noticed Mr. Payne's lamp was broken . . . There was the shattered reflector and the bits of broken bulb. The shade and lamp stand were beside the basket. He asked me to remove them. That was all. I gathered up the pieces and took them away.'

'That was at noon?' Storm repeated sharply. Goode nodded. 'Did you notice the lamp when you brought up the breakfast tray?'

'I . . . No, sir. I can't say that I did,' Goode answered.

'But don't you think you'd have noticed the wreck age if the lamp had been broken when you came up at breakfast? Don't you?'

'It would . . . seem so, sir,' Goode admitted uneasily.

'And perhaps you'd not have noticed if it had simply been in its regular position on the desk? Is that correct?'

'Yes, sir. That seems reasonable.'

Storm straightened and paced the

length of the room. 'Payne seemed much more agitated at noon, at one o'clock, than he had at breakfast. At noon the lamp was broken; no mention was made of the lamp at breakfast, nor did you notice the wreckage. Thus at noon . . . That was Saturday!' Storm remembered abruptly. He turned, a light of excitement gleaming in his eyes.

'Go downstairs and get me that salt shaker!' he ordered sharply. Goode rose and scurried from the room. Storm looked at Linda. 'What happens at noon on Saturdays?' he asked himself. 'Offices usually close!' he answered. 'A man would be free from about twelve on . . . ' He snapped his fingers. 'Everything changed at noon! Your father was worried at breakfast, Goode says. But not so acutely; it was simply the worry over the case, over you. But at noon, at one o'clock, he was extremely nervous, uneasy! Why . . . ? Because, while Goode was in Warburn, the killer had entered this house! The killer was then in this room, hiding in that closet, holding a gun on your father! From noon until he was killed, your father was at the mercy of the killer! And — '

He stopped as Goode returned, holding out a small silver salt shaker. Storm took it and turned it over. At the base was the removable plug. Carefully, Storm removed it. He emptied the salt upon the desk and spread it out. He grunted, then peered into the shaker. Linda saw his features tighten. A muted curse slipped from his lips. He jerked a pencil from the desk and poked into the shaker.

Linda saw a tiny scrap of something green tumble out. She rose swiftly, her pulse hammering, her breath forgotten. With Storm she bent over the desk as, very carefully, he lifted the scrap of thick green paper

'A scrap torn from the desk blotter here,' he whispered. She watched as he turned it over. 'There! *There!*'

Linda saw them — two penciled letters on the green paper.

The letters were: C. G.

Her eyes met Storm's and she breathed: 'Charles Gabriel!'

'Charles Gabriel,' Storm echoed softly.

'He left his office at early noon that day. He came here, hid himself in that closet with the door partly open. While your father talked with me, he knew he was to die — that was the feeling of death that was in this room. And everything he said was dictated by Gabriel! Don't you see it now — the reason for the attempted-murder lie? Your father said the killer came at nine-thirty. Where was Gabriel at nine-thirty on the evening of the twelfth . . . ? At a director's meeting of the Haliburton-Fox Corporation. A dozen reputable men would swear he was there! So he ordered your father to lie about a murder attempt at that certain time, knowing that he had a perfect alibi for nine-thirty. And he further knew that I would assume that the attempted murder and the murder itself were the actions of the same man; thus if Gabriel couldn't have attempted the murder of the twelfth, I would regard him as probably innocent of the actual killing on the thirteenth. And you!' He turned on Goode in cold quiet fury. 'With one ounce of thought or effort, you'd have found this scrap of paper that Payne managed to conceal in the shaker! But you were in such an all-fired damned hurry to get to your train — '

'Sir, I just cannot imagine how I missed it,' Goode stammered in agony. 'I am very careful, usually. I just . . . ' Goode choked. Tears welled into his eyes and he lowered his chin. 'I just filled it and . . . and tested it. The paper wasn't clogging the holes . . . '

'But why couldn't Father have done something? Just any slightest thing to warn you?' Linda asked.

'I can imagine Gabriel's threat. It involved not only your father's life, but perhaps Gabriel threatened to kill me if your father attempted a warning. Perhaps he extended the death threat to you. From my acquaintance with your father, I'd judge that he would have risked his own life, but he would never have placed another person in danger to save his own life. Do you see?'

'Yes. I . . . see,' Linda whispered. 'That was exactly like Father.'

'But I should have seen, understood!' Storm snapped. 'That shadow thing — it was so elementary, such a clear obvious impossibility. And I should have suspected Gabriel immediately — your father went to such ends to whitewash him that last afternoon. It was too apparent, and yet I muffed it! I — '

The knock on the door hushed his words. He crossed the room and turned the knob. 'Yes?' he snapped sharply.

A gleaming-eyed Dr. Shore stood there, his face tense and alive. 'That riddle of the missing garments and the mutilated side. I've got the answer, Storm! I know I've got the answer!'

'Come in,' Storm invited with a hint of mocking satisfaction. 'At long last I have the sheep. We can sharpen the long knife of proof.'

17

Shore closed the door, arched his brows questioningly at Goode. 'I would like you to lower your dress to the waist a moment, Linda,' Shore said.

'Why, I . . . Very well. Now?' she asked wonderingly.

'Please.'

She rose and glanced uncertainly about the room. Discreetly, Goode turned his back.

'If you don't mind, I'll ask Storm to bear with us,' Shore said quietly. Linda nodded slowly. She reached behind her and loosened the buttons. She shrugged out of the dress and it slipped to her waist. Shore moved forward. His fingers touched her shoulder, drawing down the strap of her slip. She was left with only her brassiere.

'Now, Storm,' Shore said crisply, 'show me exactly where the woman was scratched.'

'Here. In this region.' Linda felt his finger lightly touch her flesh. 'A rectangle, about four by five inches, around here.'

'In other words, on the flesh that is crossed by the brassiere?'

'That's right.'

'That's the region of the sixth and seventh ribs.' Shore stepped back and nodded to Linda. 'That's all, my dear.' He faced Storm. 'And you told me the woman was heard coughing?'

'I did.' Storm looked at him curiously. 'Why?'

'I am quite confident that the dead woman was afflicted with tuberculosis.'

'Tuberculosis?' Storm frowned. 'But how does that explain the mutilation on her left side?'

'Those cuts, I think, were inflicted to obliterate the needle marks made by the administration of pneumothorax. Sit down and I'll explain.'

Storm retreated to a chair. Linda finished buttoning her dress and sat down again to watch the doctor intently.

'Tuberculosis, as you know, is an infection most often found in the lungs,' he began. 'It may be confined to one, or both lungs. The basis of cure is rest for the infected lung or lungs. That's why patients with tuberculosis are nearly always ordered to bed for lengthy periods.

'When the patient is in bed, he moves less and more slowly; thus he breathes less deeply and less often. Consequently, the lung has less work to do. It can, therefore, devote more of its effort to fighting the germs of tuberculosis — walling them in, as it is called; building up calcification around the centers of infection. And the general program of resting is called 'bed-rest.'' Shore moistened his lips.

'But, in many cases, the patient will not respond to bed-rest alone. Perhaps the case is dangerously advanced. Perhaps one lung is severely infected, while the other is not. In this case the doctor may fear that the infection will spread unless more immediate action is taken. There are a variety of reasons why a doctor will resort to treatment other than simple bed-rest. And the most common second resort is what is called 'artificial pneumothorax.' Here is what it means:

'The doctor, almost always a tuberculosis specialist, uses first a small needle to inject a local anesthetic to that section of the side which is to receive treatment. And then, using a larger needle with a hollow core, the doctor penetrates the body until the point of this hollow needle has entered the pleural cavity. That is the region between the inner layer of skin and the outer side of the lung. The lung, you might say, is like an inflated bladder suspended in this pleural cavity. When the needle point has entered the cavity, the doctor then attaches a rubber tube to the other end of the needle. Through the tube and through the needle, air is forced into the pleural cavity of the patient. And what would you expect to happen then?'

'Why, I . . . I suppose the air would push the lung down.'

'Exactly. The lung is collapsed, as we call it. Then the doctor removes the needle, leaving a tiny scar where the needle has been. He paints this tiny wound with any one of a number of suitable antiseptics — tincture of Merthiolate is one; it leaves a pinkish tint on the flesh. And that,' Shore said, 'is what is called 'artificial pneumothorax.' More loosely, it is called 'giving air to the patient.' And the lung that is collapsed does almost no work; practically the entire process of breathing is carried on by the other lung, while the collapsed lung rests, fights infection, and builds up healthy tissue.' Again Shore paused and held up a finger.

'But this collapse is not permanent. The lung has a natural inclination to expand again. And it does, gradually, by the slow process of absorbing the air in the pleural cavity. Thus it is necessary to administer the pneumothorax — give the air — frequently. During the first two or three months, it may be necessary to give air every three days to keep the lung collapsed and resting. Later on during the treatment, one pneumothorax a month may be sufficient to keep the lung down. That depends upon the patient.'

'How long does the treatment last?' Storm wondered.

'It seldom lasts less than two years. Frequently it is continued for as long as five. But the patient can often be up and around while 'taking air.' One lung is enough for his normal needs, if he conducts himself mildly. But now, to get back to the case of the woman . . . ' Shore said.

'The hollow needle that is used is fairly large. It leaves scar holes. Usually, in the course of months or a year, the scars vanish. Sometimes they remain, depending on the type of skin. But it can be safely assumed that anyone taking pneumothorax will always have five or six of the needle scars on his side — that is, so long as the process is going on. As I said, these scars will be in the region you pointed out on Linda, and likely will have been painted with some antiseptic that leaves a pink tint on the skin. Third, since the pneumothorax is administered many times, it is possible and likely that this woman in question would have worn, at one time or another, every slip and brassiere she owned — worn them to the doctor's office. Thus all slips and brassieres would have been stained with this pinkish antiseptic that rubbed off her skin. A detective, searching through her possessions, would have found this pink stain appearing on every slip and brassiere, and appearing in the same place on all of them. His curiosity would have been aroused, would it not?' Shore paused and held up a second finger.

'Then again: a detective, finding her body, might have noticed this odd patch of needle scars on her side. Medical authorities might have realized what they meant, or perhaps gone into the lung itself in an examination. Then, if difficulty was encountered in identifying the body, the detective would probably question the tuberculosis specialists who administer pneumothorax. A doctor would doubtless recognize his patient from a description, and identify her properly. Thus the detective could proceed with his case. I . . . Oh, yes! The matter of the tissues in the woman's pocket . . . It is customary for people with tuberculosis to carry disposable tissues. When they must cough or clear their throats, they use the tissue to prevent spreading of the germs.'

'I see,' Storm said slowly. 'Everything

fits . . . Of course!' he whispered explosively. 'The woman's room at the Sequin was cleaned — window, floor, bath, table, everything. That wasn't done to remove fingerprints at all. The woman had no record; the killer didn't fear identification from fingerprints. It was done to prevent discovery of tuberculosis germs. They might have been found if slides were taken, and — '

'No,' Shore said. 'Perhaps the killer thought that, but the germs won't live in the open. You would have found no germs.'

'But do many people know that? I didn't. Would the killer?'

'Probably not,' Shore agreed.

'And now I see the rest,' Storm exclaimed. 'After I found the woman's body at the well, it was stolen and taken to Darby's house. The house was fired, destroying the body. I see why now. The killer feared that an autopsy would reveal the abnormal lung, the collapsed lung. That would have led us, finally, to think of tuberculosis. So he had to destroy the body utterly. Perhaps he'd planned to move it, and hadn't had the chance. He saw me at the grave. As soon as he possibly could, he moved the body and started the fire.'

Shore cocked a quizzical brow at Storm. 'And now — you mentioned something about having found the sheep. You meant the murderer?'

'I did.'

'I trust,' Shore said drily, 'that you don't have me in mind.'

'No, Doctor. Not anymore,' Storm said with a wry smile. He looked at his watch. 'Eight-ten,' he murmured. 'How many doctors in New York administer this pneumothorax treatment?'

'No idea. I've never had a great deal to do with tuberculosis, but I can call Dr. Fritz Leghorne at his house. He's in that crowd, knows them all.'

'Do that now, please,' Storm said quietly. He gazed thoughtfully after Shore as the man left the room. Presently Linda heard the click of the receiver of the hall telephone. She looked at Storm. His eyes were narrow, gleaming with a distant and speculative light.

Linda heard Shore speaking to Dr. Leghorne. Then he called, 'I need a pencil and paper, Storm.'

The detective vanished into the hall. A few moments later, Linda heard Shore slowly speaking: 'Dr. Ray Harley on West Seventy-Fourth . . . Philip Camini on Park Avenue . . . Joseph Link on Madison . . . ' The voice droned on for what seemed an eternity, then Shore spoke more crisply: 'Thanks greatly, Fritz. Goodbye.' The receiver clicked down.

'Here is the list,' Shore said. 'Do you want to call them?'

'No. If you get a nibble, I'll take the phone. You know what we're trying to find. The woman was about forty, brown hair and eyes, rather stiff and rigid in posture. She might have worn a lilac-scented perfume. Her diction was noticeably good. She was killed on the night of May the sixth, so naturally she's kept no appointments since then. The treatment you mentioned was administered to the left side. In her bag is a black dress with a white collar and white sleeves, or cuffs. The doctor might remember that. I — '

'That should be enough,' Shore decided.

'Call me when you find something.' Storm's steps moved along the hall. 'Elsie!' he called loudly.

Linda heard footsteps downstairs. 'Yes?' the girl answered.

'Come up here,' he said. Her heels clicked swiftly up the stairs. They stopped, and Linda heard a muted exchange of whispers. The telephone receiver clicked again. Shore was speaking to the Warburn operator. Storm passed the hall door, and Linda heard him open the door into the bedroom where Walt lay.

'Do you feel like getting up a minute, Gordon?' she heard the detective ask.

'Uh . . . ? Oh. Oh, I feel all right, I think.'

'In the next room,' Storm said. A few moments passed, then Storm and Walt entered. Linda smiled anxiously at her tired-eyed, robe-clad husband.

'Sit down. It won't be long,' Storm said quietly. He closed the hall door. He frowned a moment before he spoke. 'I asked you before. I want to ask again: Did you get even the slightest glimpse of the person who slugged you in Goode's bathroom?'

Walt shook his head slowly. 'Not a damn bit, Storm,' he said heavily.

'Do you remember where Charles Gabriel was when you went to that bathroom?'

Walt paused and scowled. 'I can't swear,' he said finally. 'He had been in the room. He could have been sitting there with the others. I just didn't notice.'

Storm nodded absently. He paced the length of the room. 'But you can't be sure he was there?' Storm asked. 'In the living room, I mean.'

'No. I can't swear.'

'I've got the room ready,' Elsie called from the hall.

Storm crossed the room and opened the door.

'The living room?' he asked. She nodded.

'I think it will be all right,' she said.

'Go out and tell Reddy to bring them in. Take them to the living room. I'll be down soon.'

Elsie nodded and left. For a few

moments the room was silent, and Linda could hear Shore's voice echoing from the hall: ' . . . brown hair and eyes . . . about forty . . . pneumothorax on the left . . . Nothing doing . . . ? Well, thanks, Dr. Hanson . . . '

Walt blinked at Linda, then at Storm. 'Is something about to happen?' he asked.

Storm seemed to wake from a distant half-dream. He looked at his watch, then gazed at the window. It was eight-thirty. The world outside was dark. 'Yes,' he answered. 'Something is about to happen. If you feel like dressing a little, you can join us downstairs.'

'Hell, yes, I'll come,' Walt said. 'I'd come down if I had to crawl.'

'It is one thing to be a good detective,' Storm said distantly. 'It's quite another to be a good psychologist. I used to think I was both. Tonight, and in the closing of this case, I'm not sure any more.'

Walt frowned. 'You mean your solution doesn't fit psychologically?'

'No. My solution is finally complete in every detail. I have been blind at times, stupid at others. But I doubt that many people would have done much better, and much of what has happened was necessary to my conclusion. Each step, however false, has cast another light upon the killer's prism until now, at last, it is completely illuminated. So nothing has been completely wasted, and much has been saved. But . . . ' He paused, and sighed. 'I have a fault of talking,' he said drily. 'It's time to go.' He opened the door and looked at Linda questioningly. 'You coming down now, or later with Walt?'

She started to rise, then glanced at Walt.

'I'll be only a minute,' he said. 'We'll be down then.'

Storm nodded and the door closed behind him and Goode. Their footsteps faded down the stairs. Walt nodded to Linda. They left the room and entered Linda's bedroom. He closed the door, slipped off his robe, and began to dress quickly.

Linda sat down. From the hall came the weary drone of Dr. Shore's voice. From the distant living room came the muted murmur of other voices. Linda turned her eyes back toward Walt. He was slipping into his coat. He began to comb his hair.

She watched him, and suddenly she felt the beginning of a quiet peace stealing through her mind. They were here together, and it was ending downstairs. There was only an hour left now. She felt as though some door had opened in a cell of blackness, and only moments waited until she would leave the cell. She held the thought close as she watched Walt. It was as though he had been a shadow through the days just passed; now she was awakening to him again. Suddenly, a wave of choking relief welled into her throat. She had to speak. She felt tears film her eyes.

'It's over! Think, Walt! It's over!' she sobbed. 'Tomorrow there'll be only you and me, and none of this between us! Tomorrow ... And, Walt, we'll never speak of it again! We'll promise each other.'

'Never again,' he agreed quietly. He adjusted his tie, and opened the door. 'Let's go, darling.'

'Please, kiss me, Walt! Once, quickly, now.'

He smiled. His smooth lean fingers touched her chin. His lips came down to hers. For a moment she clutched him close.

'It's time to go now,' he said.

They moved down the hall, past Shore, and down the stairs. They reached the lower hall. From beyond the closed door of the living room, a voice was speaking slowly.

'Wait just a second,' Walt said softly. He hesitated. He tilted his head. 'Strange,' he whispered. 'I can't understand — '

'What?'

'I don't know. Let's see.' He tiptoed toward the kitchen. His fingers tightened on Linda's. They moved to the sunporch. Outside was the darkness of night. 'It's out there,' Walt whispered suddenly. 'The garage!'

'But I don't hear ... don't see anything,' Linda said.

'It's out there. Move quietly,' he whispered. His fingers led her on, from the sunporch, across the wide gravel driveway, to the double garage. He touched the sliding door. Without a sound he edged it open.

Linda saw nothing save the deeper darkness within the door, nor did she hear a sound as Walt drew her inside. She did not breathe. The tense silence of him was like a bond about her throat. And then the door slid shut again. A long moment passed. Then came a tiny click, and the bright beam of a small flashlight sprayed across the darkness to catch her full in its focus, blinding her for an instant. She blinked.

'What . . . Walt, is that your light?' she breathed.

'Don't be afraid, darling,' his voice, low and musical, murmured in her ears. 'We're going now.'

'Walt! What is it? You sound so . . . you . . . your eyes . . . ' Her words faded. Her eyes became accustomed to the light, and in the glow she saw his black eyes burning. She saw the mocking smile that lay like a restless line across the still white of his face, and suddenly the face was strange — foreign and unknown. She stumbled backward one step. His fingers, stiff and hard, held her.

'No, darling, we're not going back. I can never go back, and neither shall you.' Still it was there — a musical taunting in his soft words; a raw, chill fatalism edged with loneliness.

'But . . . Walt! What kind of joke is this! What are you doing to me?' she breathed.

'It's a joke without humor, my darling. And I'm taking you with me. A letter is on the dresser of your bedroom. Storm will find it. It warns him that you will be killed if he sends the police out looking for me.'

'I . . . will . . . be . . . killed . . . ' she echoed. 'You . . . Then you . . . You . . . ' Then her words were lost in the terrifying flash of understanding.

'Oh, God! You! *You! You* — ' Her words broke. She screamed. Again she screamed. She turned. She plunged. His steel-like fingers dragged her back. She had one glimpse of his smile, then the white fist came streaking across the light and burst against her lips. Sick, hot blood filled her throat. A tempest roared into her head. There was nothing, then . . .

18

The rebirth of consciousness came like a play of lights on the horizon of night, like reflections of lightning thrown up against a sky of turmoil. They brought a restless tension to Linda's mind, and her body began to respond. She began to feel — warmth, heat, pain. She felt the weight of some grotesque burden that loaded down her mind. Then her eyes blinked open.

She was staring upward at a yellow mist. The mist shaped itself into a pattern, becoming the naked light from an oil lamp. A ceiling of stained brown paper took form. There were walls of the same dirty brown. There was an odor of dust, of stale air. There was a knife-like pain in her temples, and a salty thirst in her throat. She stared, tried to remember.

This was no place she had ever seen . . . She moved slightly. Pain fired through her temples, blinding her for an instant, sending needles of nausea through her stomach. She lay back, breathing hard, her eyes closed. At last she moved again. She found the edge of the bed on which she lay, pulled herself into a sitting position. She opened her eyes slowly on the harsh yellow mist again.

She saw a table, worn and dusty. She saw a cheap rug on the floor, an old calendar on the wall. She saw a wisp of smoke go sliding through the room. And then she saw him, sitting in a chair. A smile strayed over his lips as he watched her, holding a cigarette. His shirt was off, his chest and shoulders bare, damp with perspiration, and the black of his hair was now light blond.

'Good evening, darling,' he murmured softly.

'Walt . . . You . . . ' she whispered brokenly. She stopped. Some corner of her mind was striving to help her remember. This was Walt, but it wasn't, she realized in confusion. There had been something —

Then she saw the squat black gun on the table, the flashlight beside it. She felt

318

her mind pierce back through the curtain of blankness, and she remembered. Her fingers slipped to her neck. She felt her eyes grow wide and wider, felt the breath turn chill in her throat. And still he smiled as he slouched deep in the chair, watching her with glowing eyes.

'I suppose you may as well scream now, and learn that it does no good,' he suggested. He gestured languidly. 'We are in New York. Save for us and the usual rats, this is a vacant building. But scream if you wish.'

'You . . . killed my father,' Linda whispered.

'Don't echo the obvious, darling,' he said. 'That's too reminiscent of Gabriel.' He rose, dropped the gun into the pocket of his trousers, and crossed the room to peer into a broken piece of mirror. He touched his hair experimentally, parted it to study the roots. He turned to face her again. 'Scarcely an improvement, wouldn't you say?'

Linda hardly heard his words. She kept staring at his eyes.

'Why are we here?' she asked stonily.

'What are you doing?'

'We are here because Dr. Shore was so damnably accurate in his deduction of tuberculosis. It was a matter of a few more phone calls before he'd have contacted the right doctor; I overheard the list he was to call. And you are here in what one might call the role of a pawn.' He lit another cigarette and gazed at her appraisingly. 'My hair will soon be dry. I'll cut it. I'll have to change clothes. And then, at twenty minutes after midnight, I shall use this.' From his pocket he drew a slip of paper and held it up between two fingers. 'It's a ticket on the twelve-twenty train to St. Louis. But all of this required time, of course. Had I come alone, Storm would doubtless have enlisted the aid of the police in arresting me. As it is, I rather doubt that he will make so foolish a gesture. So, you understand?' He arched a brow and smiled. 'Simply a matter of caution.'

'But I just can't understand!' Linda stammered. 'You . . . You . . . *You!* Of everyone in that house, *you!*'

Walt laughed gently. 'A photographer

would enjoy you now. The bride in anguish, her illusions cast out upon — '

'Stop it! Don't say that!' Linda screamed. Her fingers clutched her throat. She rose. She grasped the bed, swaying as nausea welled in her throat. She closed her eyes and gasped. 'Sick . . . I'm going to be ill . . . '

'It's quite all right, darling. Merely the normal feminine reaction, isn't it?' He gestured slightly. 'I apologize for the accommodations. But, after all, this is only a vacant shirt factory; we can't expect too much.'

Slowly the nausea left her, congealing into a still and rigid stoniness, and she opened her eyes again. Now he was seated. The mirror was before him. He was plucking his eyebrows into a thin, arching pair of lines. He seemed completely oblivious to her presence.

'Why?' Linda heard her lips asking the inevitable flat question. 'Why did you do it? Why?'

Walt grinned into the mirror. 'Of course, you would ask that.' He frowned as he plucked. 'But I don't think you'll understand,' he said musingly. 'I don't think you *could*, because you've always had what you wanted. Now, Darby would make a more appreciative audience . . .

'However, to fill in the awkward conversational gap while I change my appearance, I'll try to bridge the gap of our little worlds. My name is really Herman Barty. I was born not far from here, in a tenement house in Hell's Kitchen. My father died while holding up a delicatessen place on Eighth Avenue when I was nine. My mother served three years for shoplifting. Considering that background, I'm not displeased with what I've made of myself. I'm not a bad pianist. I know some French. My manners are rather good. I'm not unattractive — or so you've told me, darling. And the wealthy ask little else.'

Linda swallowed. 'So 'Walter Gordon' is just a name . . . '

'Oh, there *was* a Walter Gordon,' he went on lightly. 'I met him two years ago when we were both in Mexico City. It was one evening in the Paloma Bar. We saw each other, were startled by the close resemblance between us. We introduced ourselves, had a drink, another. He was a lonely chap.'

He stopped, laid aside the mirror, and leaned back to light a cigarette. 'Gordon had been born in Texas, the son of a rancher. His parents were dead. He was alone, without relatives, and rather shy. He was on his way back to the States after a trip through Central and South America. He was a virtually unknown pianist who'd been searching for folk tunes of that hemisphere. I rather enjoyed him; he was a wistful, friendless fellow. I saw him several times in the next few days; he had a one-room shack where he was living. And then he became ill — appendicitis, I think. I stayed with him during those three days. I was with him when he died. It was during that time that I learned so much about him; he was afraid, I suppose, and it was lonely, dying down there in a place so strange. He told me all about his life, all he'd done, the fact that he was alone in the world, that he'd never made close friends. He'd not been back to Texas in many years. He told me of the inheritance from his father.' Walt gestured, and the cigarette left its trail of smoke in the wake of his slender hand. 'When he died, I took the notes he had made on the folk tunes. I took his identification and left mine. I returned to this country as Walter Gordon, the young unknown pianist.'

'Why did you?' Linda wondered slowly.

'Oh, for the same reason I had gone to Mexico, my dear,' he said. He rose, crossed the room, and picked up a pair of scissors. He returned to the chair, leaned the piece of mirror against the upended flashlight on the table, and raised the scissors to his hair. The blades bit into the yellow waves, and the hair showered onto his bare, damp shoulders.

'I suppose I should call it the Jessica Morgan affair,' he went on after a time. 'You wouldn't have liked her. She was fat, neurotic, sentimental; the widow of a man who had done well indeed in the shirt-making business. I was her butler. Oh, yes.' He glanced up and his eyes twinkled. 'I owe much of my sophistication to my years of servitude. And eventually my relationship with Jessica became rather favored. You must remember she was sixty, and a man hadn't quite ceased to interest her. It called for the mildest of caresses. A kiss on her throat, a — '

'Don't! It's loathsome! Vile! It — ' Linda choked.

'You think of morality, darling, while I, being more practical, think of money. You've never lived in Hell's Kitchen,' he said with gentle reproof. 'But she was repulsive. It came to the point where I could no longer stomach her. Then I made my one mistake — I listened to the stupid maid. Her name was Helen Cory — a thin, slatternly woman who'd been with Jessica for years. And she, even as you and Jessica, was hungry for love . . . ' Walt smiled indulgently. Linda's fingers opened and closed on her throat.

'Yes? Even as I,' she whispered strangely.

'I rather think that Helen deliberately deceived me,' Walt mused aloud. 'She told me that someday she would have a great deal of money — that Jessica had made her the sole heir in a will . . . Looking back on it now, I wonder why I believed her so readily. Perhaps I just hated Jessica. But, anyway, I married the maid. That was nearly three years ago. We didn't tell Jessica. We kept working at her apartment. And, very slowly, very carefully, a little at a time, I poisoned her. She died. Her will was read. And Helen, my dear, stupid wife, received the magnificent sum of five thousand dollars!' He stabbed out his cigarette and his eyes blazed. A crooked mirthless smile twisted his lips and he laughed softly. 'Five thousand dollars! And I, in the investigation that followed, found it necessary to go to Mexico. There I met Walter Gordon. There he died, and with him died Herman Barty, the butler who had poisoned Jessica Morgan.'

Linda leaned forward and breathed jerkily. 'But didn't . . . didn't you *kill* him?' she whispered. '*Didn't* you?'

'Ah, now your intuition wakes. You're rather attractive with your cheeks soiled, pale, with your eyes alive again. I — '

'*Didn't* you kill him? Tell me! You killed

the real Walt Gordon!'

'Hardly as you would expect. I merely let him die,' Walt said with a deprecating gesture. 'When he became ill, I suspected an infected appendicitis. It was only natural for me to toy with the advantages of his death. As I've said, we were remarkably alike in appearance. We both played the piano. He had spoken often of the fact that he had no friends, no relatives; that he'd never been close to anyone. More and more I appreciated the advantages of his death. Then his pains became more acute. At times he was delirious. He called for a doctor. When he returned to a semi-lucid frame of mind, I assured him that the doctor had been there; I assured him that nothing was seriously wrong with him. Then I took the liberty of giving him several doses of a strong cathartic. I assume the appendix burst. Anyway, he died, poor fellow, and I became Walter Gordon.'

'And then . . . then you met me,' Linda breathed. Her eyes clung to his face. It was as if there was some pleasure in the torture of watching him, some strange satisfaction in hearing all he could say. His words, each of them, were hot whips of raw humiliation that at last would beat her into uncaring peace. Her fingers clenched. 'And I never was anything but another Jessica, was I? Tell me what I was! You can't hurt me anymore! You never loved me, never cared! Go on, say everything you — '

'You're becoming hysterical, Linda,' he said curtly. 'If possible, let's not be maudlin. Nor was it so simple as merely 'meeting you,' as you put it. You fail to give me credit for the months of planning, thinking, rounding out of my background. There was endless practicing on the piano, studying of Gordon's notes on folk tunes, events of his travels. I had to formulate a consistent character and learn to live it. I became a faintly impractical, quiet-mannered musician. But I needed an entree. Ah! To lecture at women's clubs in the wealthy districts near New York! Perfect! It required only a glib tongue, a confident manner, a certain charm, good looks. The ladies, as you know, darling, judge a man on little things. And it was the ladies, the wealthy ladies, I was seeking. For they,' he said with a gentle smile, 'are the world's greatest fools.' He paused a moment, his dark eyes thoughtful. 'Anyway, there is something crude and prosaic about a pattern involving only men. A stupid thief steals from a man; an extortionist selects a wealthy man. I have no interest in men. Crime, in its ideal form, can cease to be crime at all, don't you think?' He arched a brow. 'With some lovely lady, it ascends to the plane of delicacy. It is refined, quiet — '

'You are *insane!*' Linda whispered.

'Oh, come. Don't resort to clichés. I'm no more insane than you are. I've simply reduced my ambitions to simple reality. My means of achievement are, shall we say, unconventional. That's all there is to it.' He looked at his watch, then lifted the mirror and studied his short-cropped blond hair. He began to use the scissors again.

'It seemed ideal,' he continued in a pleasant, half-detached tone. 'I met you. You are quite attractive, darling, and rather childlike too. I confess I was beginning to feel a genuine affection. But . . . ' He sighed lightly and tilted the mirror. 'The past has a sardonic permanence, Linda. We pass it by, yet it remains. It returns, like some odor on an ill wind. In my case, amid my plans, it was Helen, the stupid, slatternly maid I had married. I had to kill her.'

He laid down the scissors and faced Linda. His eyes again were deep and flashing. She felt their invisible lash.

'She was Helen Walker? She was the woman in the well-grave?'

'She was,' he said vibrantly. 'Damn her forever!'

19

He rose and prowled the length of the room. Veins grew into livid cords at his temples. For the first time, Linda glimpsed the boiling fury within him. It raised and shook his voice as he spoke:

'Millions of people in New York! And of them all, which one must I meet! Her! *Again!* It was in an elevator in an office building on Fifth Avenue, the morning of April the first, two months ago. I walked into the damned elevator. It was crowded. I didn't see her until the door was closed, until she threw her arms around me.' He was tense, his face strained with the torment of recollection.

'She began to babble, sob before everyone. The maudlin imbecility of the fool! She thought I'd come back to her — that I'd come to that building searching, knowing she'd be there. Then she turned and introduced me to a man — a Dr. Marlin Grove. She introduced me as Herman, the husband she'd been telling him so much about. I was *trapped* in that damned elevator. I had to face the devil, keep a straight face. I had to go with them to Grove's office. That's where Helen was headed. It was that or make a scene.'

He stopped. His eyes blazed. His fingers opened and closed convulsively. 'But for that one day, that one chance meeting, Storm would never have learned the truth. That meeting and that woman — they were the cause of it all,' he panted.

He snatched a cigarette from his pack and lit it. He paced the room again. 'Grove is a tuberculosis specialist. Helen had had a hemorrhage a year before. An examination had revealed tuberculosis in the left lung. For a year she'd been an invalid under Grove's care. That day she received pneumothorax at his office. Then, privately, Grove called me aside and talked to me. He said he was glad I'd come back; he said Helen would need care and help for a long time. He was a shrewd man; I could see him appraising me, judging, wondering where I'd been. God knows what Helen had told him about me. At last we got out of the damned place. Helen was sobbing and babbling again about how glad she was I was back, wanting to know where I'd been, why I'd stayed so long. I had to keep her quiet, try to avoid suspicion. I went with her to her dismal little room on Seventh Avenue. It . . . Oh, God, it was revolting!' He hurled down the cigarette and raked his fingers through his hair.

'There we were in that cell-like room. She had to undress and go to bed. Grove allowed her to be up only three hours a day. But she lay there holding my hand. Oh, yes! She had to hold my hand! She had to tell me every sordid detail of the whole business. Her hemorrhage, how she'd gone to Grove, how her money had given out. They were giving her the room where she stayed. She cried over Grove and his kindness; she hadn't been able to pay her bill. But now everything was going to be perfect. Here I was, back. And didn't I still have the five thousand dollars that Jessica had left her? Or even more, perhaps? Oh, everything was going to splendid — she could almost feel herself getting well. Then she wanted to know why I hadn't written her, where I'd been. Again I heard the details of the damned disease, even to seeing the needle scars on her side. It was after ten that night before I could get away. I told her I was going after food. That was the night I didn't meet you at Shalo's.'

'That night . . . while I waited . . . you were with that woman you married . . . the woman you later killed,' Linda breathed jerkily.

'And had it not been for that one day, that one minute in the elevator, I wouldn't be hiding, fleeing tonight!' he almost shouted. 'I had known you over a year then. We were engaged. It was only a matter of weeks until . . . ' He stopped. He exhaled heavily and shrugged. 'As I said, my darling, the past has a sardonic permanence. See where we are tonight. Think where we might have been . . . '

'I am thinking of just that,' Linda said.

'You have regained your admirable self-possession,' he said, smiling. 'But you haven't asked me about the murder of your father . . . '

'It isn't self-possession,' she said quietly. 'You want me to beg. At last I begin to understand just a little of you, Walt, Herman, whoever you are. I called you insane. I was wrong; you're perfectly sane, but you're a monster of cruelty. You want to tell me about the murder. Tell me, then! Tell me how you killed him! *Tell me!*' She blinked tears away.

He gazed at her. 'Only the rich — after they are rich — can indulge in the gentler virtues, darling.' He sat down and his eyelids lowered sleepily. He folded his arms across his bare chest. 'You may remember, it was the night of May the fourth, a Thursday, when Helen first visited your father. You and I attended a show in Warburn that night. When we returned, when we entered the hall at your house, I smelled that lilac perfume. Instantly, I suspected that Helen had been there — she always used the stuff to vulgar excess. And I suspected why she'd been there. But when your father came downstairs, he was his usual cordial and natural self. I watched him closely. I saw not the slightest hint that he even suspected the truth about me. Not then, at any rate; later, I thought that perhaps he was beginning to suspect me. I am a reasonably good psychologist, Linda. Your father was too frank to pose so well. So I concluded that Helen had made no revelations. But I knew she had traced me. I knew she would have to die.' He sighed.

'That night, I went from your house to her little room in New York. She was gone; her things were gone. But in the wastebasket I found a newspaper about ten days old. In the pictorial section I found candid pictures taken on the opening night of the dog show in Madison Square Garden. There was a picture of us in our box. Beneath the picture were our names, Linda Payne and Walter Gordon, 'the pianist and lecturer.' Our engagement and approaching marriage was mentioned. So Helen knew . . . Now she had left her room. It was bound to be blackmail. How would I find her?' He arched a brow. 'Wouldn't she be

going back to Dr. Grove's office?' He
smiled. 'And she *did* — the very next day.
I was watching. I followed her when she
left. She entered a cigar store and went to
a phone booth. I entered the adjoining
booth. I heard her call your father, ask to
see him again, arrange the hours. I
followed her to the Sequin. I decided she
wouldn't make the trip to Warburn that
night, since Grove allowed her to be up
only three hours a day and she had
already made a trip to his office. It would
be the next night, or the night after that, I
decided. So . . . That night, I had dinner
at your house. I feigned illness, remember? I borrowed a thermometer. You
didn't know I had held that thermometer
under warm water to fake a temperature.
I wanted an alibi of illness for the next
few nights. Then I left, came into New
York. I got old clothes that couldn't be
identified as mine. I bought thick glasses
at a pawnshop. The next afternoon, I
called you to tell you I was staying in bed.
Then, wearing the old clothes and
glasses, I went to the vicinity of the
Sequin and took up my watch. At

seven-forty she left the Sequin and went to Grand Central Station. She took a train for Warburn, as did I.' He paused to smile wryly and light a cigarette. He leaned forward, his eyes now bright and dancing with restless light. He was speaking in soft, swift whispers:

'I followed her to the driveway of your house. There I killed her with a heavy cane I'd carried for that purpose. I did not, unfortunately, notice the loss of that shoulder ornament . . . I carried her body to the creek. I waded along the creek to break my trail. I took the body to the abandoned well. I saw the light at Darby's house. I crept up there to assure myself I was safe; I saw him lying unconscious on the floor. I did not, unfortunately, see Brill.

'I returned to the well. I knew an identification of Helen would lead, almost certainly, to Dr. Grove. And he had seen me with her. I knew he distrusted me; it had been in his eyes, his manner. So I had to remove the scars of her disease. I cut the flesh about the needle scars. I removed her slip and brassiere that were

338

stained with antiseptic. I knew that her face, by virtue of my cane, would never be identified. I buried her and went down the lane toward Hamondville. At the vacant filling station, I changed into my customary clothes and started the fire that was to destroy Helen's purse, underwear, and my working clothes, so to speak. I assure you, I was unaware Brill was following me. I know now, of course, that he salvaged her identification card from her unburned purse, traced her to her room where she'd taken me, learned of her disease and of Grove, and then visited Grove probably. By careful questioning Brill learned what I looked like; he fitted me into the pattern. Grove did not learn the truth. Brill, as he told Storm, had other plans for me. But so much for Helen.' He rose and mashed out his cigarette.

'Your father called Storm into the case,' he continued. 'I had the notion that your father's suspicion was finally gravitating toward me. I couldn't be sure. After all, it was only natural for me to be apprehensive, and there were so many clues that

Helen *might* have left in his mind the day she saw him — small things that might have grown into significance as he thought about them. And anyway, darling, your father was a far shrewder man than you are a woman. To deceive you until your fortune was manipulated would be easy. With him alive and watchful, it would be difficult. I dislike difficulties.

'I chose my time — the afternoon of Saturday the thirteenth. I chose it for certain reasons. I realized, first, that I'd have a perfect alibi for nine-thirty of the previous evening; I was going to be attending a theater with you, my dear. Thus, if Storm never found a flaw in the attempted-murder tale, I'd have a perfect alibi. On the other hand if, as I suspected and planned, Storm did learn that the attempted-murder story was a lie and that your father was under duress the day of his death, I planned to have Storm focus his suspicion on Gabriel, and not on me. I'd take care of that . . . I'd seen in the *Wall Street Journal* — which I read regularly, my dear, because of interest in certain valuable securities which seemed destined to be yours and then mine — that Gabriel would attend a directors' meeting of the Haliburton-Fox Corporation on the evening of the attempted murder. He, too, would have a perfect alibi. Thus, when Storm learned that your father had lied about the nine-thirty attack, he would wonder why. He'd realize that both Gabriel and I had perfect alibis for that time. His suspicion would be aroused. Then, as I carefully planned, Storm would uncover proof that incriminated Gabriel.'

Walt gestured casually. 'Before dawn on the morning of the thirteenth, I dressed in old clothes and took the train to your house. I arrived before anyone was awake. I forced an entrance into the house and awakened your father with my gun. I explained to him how matters stood. He had the choice of obeying my orders, or of violating them and risking the consequences to himself and others. You, for instance . . . He accepted the orders.'

'Of course,' Linda breathed. 'You *would* use that.'

'Of course,' he echoed lightly. 'I had

calculated your father's decision perfectly. I gave him the first . . . suggestions. I told him he would remain in his room that morning. And, suspecting that Goode would notice some change in your father's manner, I instructed your father to mention his worry and nervousness. I removed his gun from his desk and unloaded it. I warned him to limit his movements so that I could always see him from the closet. I reminded him of the possible consequences of any disobedience: his death and Goode's . . . Then Goode came up to call your father to breakfast. Following my orders, your father ate in his room. I advised your father on his plans to go into New York, and likewise on his plans to give Goode a vacation, starting that afternoon.' Walt gestured slightly and lit another cigarette.

'When Goode came to remove the breakfast tray, your father informed him of the 'plans.' Also, he told Goode he intended on taking a walk that morning; I wanted it to seem that your father was perfectly free to move about as he wished. So . . . Goode drove into Warburn. At the point of a gun, your father made two phone calls. One was to Storm's office, asking Storm to come to Warburn. The other was to Gabriel, asking him to prepare a new will that afternoon — a will in which you, Linda, would be the sole beneficiary. When the will was ready, Gabriel was to bring it out to your father. And you wonder why?' he asked.

'First, I wanted someone upon whom to cast guilt *in the event that* the suicide scene was not accepted; naturally, I doubted that it would be. Too much had happened; Storm knew too much background. Almost certainly, a murderer was going to be needed. Gabriel was my selection . . . Thus I had your father ask him to remain at the office that Saturday afternoon and work, knowing the office would probably be empty and Gabriel would encounter difficulty in proving his whereabouts. Secondly, I wanted the will to be in a state of flux at the time of the murder, because I knew one of two things would happen: either Gabriel would produce the new will which gave you, and thus me, everything; or Gabriel would seek to conceal the new will and save his share of your father's estate. If he chose the second course, he would play directly into my hands, for I had your father write a letter to Gabriel after making the phone call. That was the letter that Storm found. And,' Walt said smugly, 'I had judged Gabriel accurately. He didn't reveal the new will. At no time has he mentioned that new will. Gabriel, I fear, is a little less than honorable himself.' He yawned and stretched.

'Then, while Goode was in Warburn, I forced your father to accompany me downstairs. We opened the front door and arranged the walking stick. I had him dress. I broke the lamp and put the pieces in the wastebasket. I ordered your father to appear much more nervous and ill-at-ease. He obeyed. Presently Goode brought up the lunch tray and train ticket. He was asked to remove the broken lamp. Later, Goode returned to remove the lunch tray. At two o'clock, Storm arrived. I had instructed your father carefully on this scene.

'I told him that any disobedience of my

instructions would result in his death and Storm's. As an additional point of persuasion, I told him that only with his cooperation would your life be safe. Allow me to carry out my plans, I said, and you would enjoy only an undesirable marriage. Or suffer it, if you prefer the word,' he said drily. 'Otherwise, I said, you would be killed. It was, to use a trite phrase, a bargain between hell and damnation. He could not take the risk of disbelieving me. He took my orders . . .

'I coached him on the story of the fake murder attempt, setting the time at nine-thirty the evening before. I ordered him to be emphatic in his trust of Gabriel, hoping thereby to turn Storm's suspicion that way. Psychology of a sort,' he said lightly. 'I had him write Storm a check for future services. You see, I felt I would be able to manipulate myself into Storm's good graces, while the police were something quite different. In short, all your father said and did that day was in obedience to my . . . Why are you frowning?'

'Why did you have to incriminate

Gabriel?' she asked heavily.

'Oh, don't be dense, darling. That was a perfectly normal and essential part of the scheme. As I said before, there was almost no chance that the suicide scene would be accepted by Storm. On the other hand, an obvious murder would definitely involve the police. So I would make it *look* like suicide, but leave enough proof behind for Storm to be able to make a case against Gabriel. You must remember, Linda, a murderer was needed.' He smiled and gestured.

'Thus everything I ordered your father to do that day was calculated to form a pattern of guilt upon Gabriel. I had your father appear only mildly nervous during the morning. I had him appear much more agitated in the afternoon when, presumably, Gabriel would have had a chance to leave his office on Saturday. I had, further, arranged for Gabriel to be occupied in his office, where, I hoped, he would be alone — without proof of his whereabouts. I had your father select nine-thirty as the time of the false murder attempt, because Gabriel had a board meeting at that time. Thus, if Storm learned that your father had been lying, had been under duress that afternoon, he would begin to weigh the items in your father's false story. He would ask himself why your father had chosen that particular time — nine-thirty. Naturally, Storm would think, it was because the killer had a perfect alibi for that time. Of course, I had an alibi for that time, but I would be rejected as a suspect as the bulk of proof mounted against Gabriel . . . Presently Storm would learn that the lamp had been unbroken at breakfast, but was in pieces at lunch — a definite indication that your father had lied about the murder attempt of the previous evening. And, presently, Goode would remember your father's odd mention of the salt shaker. Storm would inspect the shaker. There he would find the scrap of blotter I had initialed with the letters C. G. Thus his proof would be almost conclusive. Gabriel might not be able to *prove* he'd been at his office during Saturday afternoon.

'His story of the changed will would

seem just a weak alibi. Further, you will recall that I'd had your father ask Gabriel to bring the new will out that Saturday afternoon; thus it would probably be proved that Gabriel was in the vicinity of your father's house around the time of the murder. And then, as a last detail, I left a half-smoked cigar of Gabriel's brand in the tray at your father's room after the murder. That was designed to point instantly to Gabriel. But, as irony would have it, the cigar was removed. Storm was delayed in focusing his hard suspicion on Gabriel; Goode forgot the salt-shaker episode until this evening. The entire course of the case, as I had planned it, was disrupted by that man Brill and his nonsense with Darby. In fact, my dear, had I known of Darby's situation, I might have selected him as my guilty party. But we never know everything,' he said drily. He looked at his watch and straightened.

'It is late. The other details were functional, or they were products of immediate necessity . . . After killing your father, I hurried back to New York and had dinner with Storm. I showed great concern for your safety. Storm, knowing I had a perfect alibi for the time of the attempted murder, was inclined to trust me. As he revealed some details of your danger, I became most upset. I announced I was going to join you, marry you at once. An ideal arrangement, naturally,' the killer said. He picked up a clean shirt.

'As your husband, I would be safer from immediate suspicion. I would be in the bosom of the case, able to follow all developments, to protect myself if need be. And, lastly, darling, I would have made a marriage to a very lovely lady and a by-no-means-unlovely fortune. So . . . I joined you in El Paso. We were married. Then came the notice of your father's death. We returned. Constantly I assumed the role of watchful protector. The discovery of Helen's body posed a danger, but I overcame that. Then came the ill-fated appearance of Brill. It was necessary for me to cause the fire, hurry to the downstairs bath, shoot Brill, and short-out the lights before — '

'I wonder that you didn't shoot Storm,' Linda said slowly.

'You're being emotional instead of thoughtful, darling. Brill was the tongue that held my secret, while Storm was simply the ear that was listening to learn. Silence the tongue, and the ears can listen forever and learn nothing. But, anyway, with Brill dead, I was not secure anymore. How much had he told Storm . . . ? I could not be sure. And when I was moved to Goode's quarters, I was apart from the scene of developments. I *had* to get back to the house — to listen, to watch, and to be ready. I hit upon the idea of slugging myself. Oh, yes, it hurt a little, but — '

'Hero!' Linda sneered.

'I forgive you, darling,' he said with a smile. 'But I *did* get back into the house. There I became the unhappy eavesdropper to my misfortune. Dr. Shore had only a half-dozen names to call before he would have contacted Dr. Grove. So . . . Well, here we are.' He spread his hands. 'A rather negative ending, isn't it, darling?'

Linda's eyes followed the arc of his arm around the lamplit walls. For a moment she stared at the heavy wooden door.

'I wouldn't think of it, darling,' the killer said. 'Oh, the door is unlocked, but we are four floors from the ground. The door downstairs is locked. The building is rather vacant and dark. It makes quite a labyrinth, I assure you.'

'What is this place? Why did we come *here*?' she whispered.

'I suppose this is the one real favor Jessica ever did me. This building was hers. For years it has been vacant, since her shirt-making husband died. A lawsuit of some kind, I think. It's hardly more than a barn, but still I knew of it, knew it was vacant. And, unlike the common run of dangerously unconventional persons, I plan for adversity as well as success. One might fail today, but tomorrow there will always be another name and scene, another gullible lady. Always have a plan, darling . . . Here I have kept a bag packed with clothes, toilet articles, a little money. You see how changed my appearance is. My destination is known to me alone, and it is almost twelve. And so, my darling,' he finished quietly, 'we seem to approach the end of our honeymoon.'

'Honeymoon,' she echoed strangely. 'I'd forgotten . . . '

'How uncomplimentary,' he chided. He lifted a plain blue tie. Deftly, he twirled a knot and drew it tight. He slipped into a neat double-breasted coat. He looked at her with grave, level eyes as he combed his hair. He fitted a pearl-gray hat to his head and glanced perfunctorily at his watch. He looked at her again. With the meeting of their eyes, Linda felt a cold deep hush in her throat.

'It has been too short, my dear,' he said quietly. 'We have been the victims of that sardonic past. I am sorry.'

'I hope . . . ' She breathed chokingly. 'I hope you will die. Soon. I've never hoped that for anyone else in my life, but I pray for it for you, Walt.'

'But the wish is not the fact, nor are all prayers answered.' A lean and slow smile stretched across his lips, showing the white of his teeth. His eyes narrowed. Behind the lashes the blackness glistened like ice in the night. His hand moved very slowly. And, as Linda watched with fixed wide eyes, the gun came up in his hand. The smile was now a frozen line across his thin red lips.

'Goodbye, darling,' the killer said quietly. 'You know what I look like now. You know too much. I repeat, darling — '

Linda closed her eyes. Her lips trembled. 'Oh, God,' she tried to whisper. 'Oh, God . . . '

20

'*That's all, Gordon.*' The words, measured and cold, filled the room. Linda saw Walt twist sharply around. And then, beyond him, she saw the open door. She saw a gun, a hand. And behind it, shadowed in the darkness beyond the door, she saw the slender, still figure of John Storm. Slowly, he came forward into the bright yellow lamplight, and the door closed behind him. 'Drop the gun, Gordon.'

There was a rasping curse from Walt, a flashing movement of his right arm, a metallic snapping sound from the gun in his hand. For a fraction of a second Linda waited for the thundering roar. It did not come. Nothing came but a strangled 'Damn!' from Walt's lips, and then the deliberate voice of Storm again:

'That gun will not fire, Gordon. I took care of that before I ever let you leave the house. Now you can — '

'You . . . You *let* me leave the house! You *knew* I . . . *Knew* I was — '

'The murderer, yes. When I called you into Payne's room, before I went downstairs, I knew you were the murderer. You were called in there to give Elsie a chance to search your bedroom and jam your gun. I knew you would try to escape. I let you escape, but I came with you. Under the turtleback of the car.'

Walt's thin face furrowed into a mask of furious terror. He hurled the gun into a corner. His shoulders hunched. Linda saw his muscles gathering. Falling to her knees, she crept along the wall, moving away from him.

'God damn you, Storm,' he whimpered thinly, his lips twitching uncontrollably. His throat swelled and heaved. 'Damn . . . damn you,' he whimpered again. It was a new tone now — weak, frightened.

Storm said, 'Don't move, Gordon! Don't touch that — '

His words were lost. Linda's eyes widened in horror as she saw Walt's eyes fixed purposefully on the lamp — the

355

only light in the room. She saw his muscles tense beneath his coat.

Then he leaped. With a wild, swinging lunge, his arm drove across the table toward the lamp. In the same instant a thundering blast burst against the walls. There was a scream of startled agony from Walt's lips, then came the crash of the lamp.

There was a brilliant flash of orange flame as the oil ignited. The flash became a small sea of flames that licked hungrily at the floor, then mounted. They cast a weird light in the room, in which Linda saw Walt staggering backward, clutching at his stomach. His face was etched with lines of agony. A tremor jerked through him, doubling him forward to his knees. And, for an instant, Linda saw the small, moist stain of darkness growing on his shirt.

She heard him choke and scream. The instant of frozen turmoil shattered. Storm's fingers were dragging her upward, lifting her into his arms. Above the angry crackle of the climbing flames, she heard the door opening. For a moment she looked back into the room, then closed her eyes against the fallen horror that she saw.

That was all she remembered.

The girl wore a simple dress of cool white linen. The soft waves of her golden-brown hair swayed to her rhythmic stride. Her eyes were clear, tinted with the color of her hair. She paused at the last door of the corridor and turned the knob. She entered the small reception room. A frank-eyed girl looked up.

'Oh, good morning, Miss Payne,' she greeted.

'Hello, Elsie. Is he in?' She nodded toward the inner door.

'Waiting. He's expecting you. Go ahead.'

Linda crossed the room, opened the inner door, and stepped into a large, plain office. Across the room, at the desk, John Storm looked up. He smiled and rose.

'Good morning. I'm glad to see you,' he said quietly. 'Sit down.' They shook hands and Linda sat down at the side of the desk. Storm looked at her steadily as he returned to his chair. 'You look very well.'

'Three weeks of rest can make a lot of difference,' Linda said. She hesitated a moment. 'I wanted to see you before . . . I'm leaving tomorrow. I'm going to Maine for the rest of the summer.'

'You'll be back in the fall?'

She nodded. 'I don't know what I'll do then. I think I want to get a job. I'll be thinking about that while I'm in Maine.'

'It's a good idea . . . How do you feel now?' he asked quietly.

'I must be terribly insensitive,' she said, 'because I don't feel nearly as tragic as I should.'

He tapped the point of a pencil on the desk blotter. 'And I wonder, Linda, if you understand why I made the choice I did? Why I let Gordon take you away in that car?'

'I think so. I . . . But how did you *know* Walt was the murderer?' she asked swiftly. 'All your evidence pointed to Gabriel then.'

'Just two details, Linda, the second of

which was absolutely conclusive, while the first merely pointed the way . . . You remember, the suspects had been narrowed down to Gabriel, Goode, and Gordon. One of them, the killer, had carried Helen Walker's body to the well-grave. Could Goode have done it? Was he physically able . . . ? Almost certainly not. That left Gabriel and Gordon. Now . . . You'll remember that Brill said the killer entered the vacant service-station by the high restroom window. Brill said that he himself used another window. Why did he choose another window? Because he couldn't get through the higher window, naturally. And if Brill, a hardened man, couldn't negotiate that window, neither could Gabriel, a sedentary office man. That left only Gordon. That was the first detail.'

'And the second? The one that was conclusive?' Linda asked.

'We knew that your father was acting under duress that last Saturday afternoon when I talked with him. Someone, we knew, was hidden in that closet. Not Goode, of course; I saw Goode leave the room. That left Gabriel and Gordon. And it would not have been Gabriel. One telltale fact gave me that answer — the answer that saved Gabriel and broke Walt Gordon.' Storm leaned forward. 'Gabriel suffers from asthma, remember. From the time he first arrived at your house Sunday morning, he began sneezing and complaining of the effects of the tulips in the hothouse. And those tulips were fifty feet from the house. But . . . But that last Saturday afternoon when I saw your father, there were three black tulips in the vase on his desk — less than ten feet from that closet. Yet I heard not the slightest sniffle or sneeze during the hour I was there. Thus Gabriel could *not* have been hiding in that closet. That left only Gordon. And that . . . that was the case.' He leaned back in his chair. Linda was nodding slowly.

'But I want you to understand why I let you go with Gordon when he fled,' Storm said deliberately. 'Had I revealed him in a routine manner, before a roomful of people, you would have heard only the facts. Eventually, of course, you would have gotten the story of his past, but it would have come slowly. At no time would you have seen him in the full naked truth of his criminal brutality — seen him as a passionate destroyer, as a man willing to destroy you. You would have seen him lying and backtracking, trying to put the best light on himself, trying to escape the full weight of his crimes.

'As his wife, it would have been almost impossible for you not to have felt some hesitant blind sympathy for him. Perhaps you would never have been entirely convinced that he was as bad as he was. You might have wondered if somewhere you had failed. Almost surely you would have felt the lasting emotional distur-bance of what we'll call a nightmare, not a marriage. But, as it was and is,' he said simply, 'you saw him for what he was. You couldn't help it. I counted on that. I didn't count on him to make it so hideous and . . . But that's all over,' he said quietly. 'He's dead. You will forget him.'

'Some day; perhaps much sooner than I think. I . . . I think you were very wise that night. I thank you.'

He smiled and shrugged. Linda hesitated and glanced at her watch. 'It's time I was going,' she said slowly. 'My train leaves at eleven.'

Storm rose with her and they moved toward the door. 'And you will be back in the fall?' he asked.

'Late in September,' she said.

He touched the knob. His fingers waited. 'I . . . I hope I'll see you then. If you wouldn't mind calling me . . . '

'I will.' Her eyes met his. 'I'll call you as soon as I get back.'

'Good.' He held out his hand. 'Goodbye, Linda.'

'Goodbye.' She felt his fingers, firm and warm on hers. The door was opening. He was smiling. She smiled back. 'I'll see you in September,' she promised.

He nodded. Their fingers parted. She stepped through the doorway. A last time their eyes met, then she turned. She walked out of the office, out of the building, into the clean, sane sunlight.